lebor ɢabála érenn

JIM FITZPATRICK

THE SILVER ARM

WRITTEN AND ILLUSTRATED BY
JIM FITZPATRICK

EDITED BY PAT VINCENT

Paper Tiger

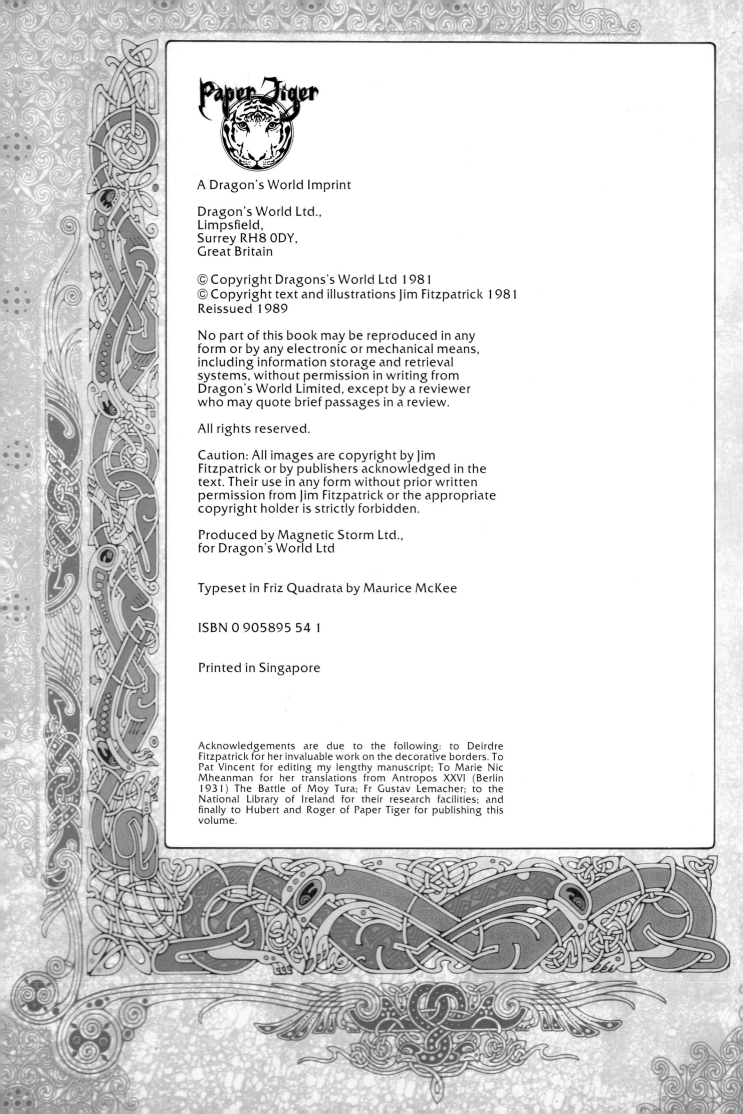

A Dragon's World Imprint

Dragon's World Ltd.,
Limpsfield,
Surrey RH8 0DY,
Great Britain

Produced by Magnetic Storm Ltd.,
for Dragon's World Ltd

Typeset in Friz Quadrata by Maurice McKee

ISBN 0 905895 54 1

Printed in Singapore

Acknowledgements are due to the following: to Deirdre
Fitzpatrick for her invaluable work on the decorative borders. To
Pat Vincent for editing my lengthy manuscript; To Marie Nic
Mheanman for her translations from Antropos XXVI (Berlin
1931) The Battle of Moy Tura; Fr Gustav Lemacher; to the
National Library of Ireland for their research facilities; and
finally to Hubert and Roger of Paper Tiger for publishing this
volume.

To Deirdre

Contents

Introduction

Writing about the inspiration of his first volume of 'The Book of Conquests' Jim Fitzpatrick said:

"It was in Clare that I, as a boy, first heard in fireside tellings the stories of the Shí or the Fairy Folk as the Tuatha Dé Danann are known today. In those legendary tales of my home countryside there was material enough for a dozen books of myth and folklore."

In this second volume, titled "The Silver-Armed Warrior", Jim Fitzpatrick resorts again to that treasure house of his Irish childhood, a cultural heritage shared and transmitted not only by Yeats and Lady Gregory but by a thousand unknown voices telling the lovingly guarded stories to countless generations of children and adults alike.

Ireland is a land of extremities. Her people have known great poverty, oppression and suffering but those treasures and monuments saved from the depradations of time, the illuminated manuscript, the ruined tower on a now deserted headland, the mysteriour rows of megaliths, the lonely cairns, bear silent testimony to a rich complexity of life and culture going back not into the mists of time but to a golden, more heroic age.

It was Yeats who said that out of change and extremity 'A terrible beauty is born'. Ireland still knows the immediacy of suffering, but the pain is the price paid for the vividness of life, the darkness against which light may leap more brightly. The culturally disinherited, the numb, the half-dead feel neither pain nor joy. It is in the face of hardship that a nation forges a sense of historical identity and guards it most jealously.

The oral tradition presents history from the inside; it preserves both the specificity of the historical moment and welds it together with the unique significance the past has for the descendants of those for whom that same moment spelt honour or shame and which, renewed within the present, gives a sharp sense of the possibilities of life as well as the certainty of mortality. Academic historians construct other truths, more remote perspectives slanted retrospectively to endorse theories of change and reality that belong to lecture theatres or studies where books block the window and the only light falls from an Anglepoise lamp.

In his version of the 'Book of Conquests' and the story of Nuada of the Silver Arm, Jim Fitzpatrick is seeking to fix the fireside story teller's voice in time, to preserve its authenticity, as scribes and scholars have done throughout the centuries and, also like them, to embelish this inscription of the mythic history of his own race with all the artistic skill and craft at his command; make it a labour of love, a personal affirmation of his cultural identity and pride.

Just as he has preserved the mythical integrity of his story yet changed the tone of its telling to enable it to resonate more fully in the mind and imagination of the present day reader, so he has kept many of the traditional graphic motifs that decorate the pages of older hand-wrought books and incorporated the traditional Celtic designs within an explosion of colour and movement that belongs unmistakably to contemporary illustration. Here is a book that will appeal to both the child and man who might otherwise pass by those earlier painted mss. as dusty museum pieces as well as to those who know by heart the illumination of the Book of Kells.

This is indeed popularisation at its best. Jim Fitzpatrick has taken his heritage and, by giving it the print of his individuality and talent, made it excitingly accessible to those who might ever have remained ignorant of the glorious past and vivid present of what is too easily dismissed as something belonging to a remote time: the Celtic spirit, its bravery and its pride, which still leaps from these pages with as much sinew and beauty as those ancient heroes lept across the battle fields of Éireann.

Pat Vincent.

PART ONE

THE TRANSFORMATIONS OF TUAN

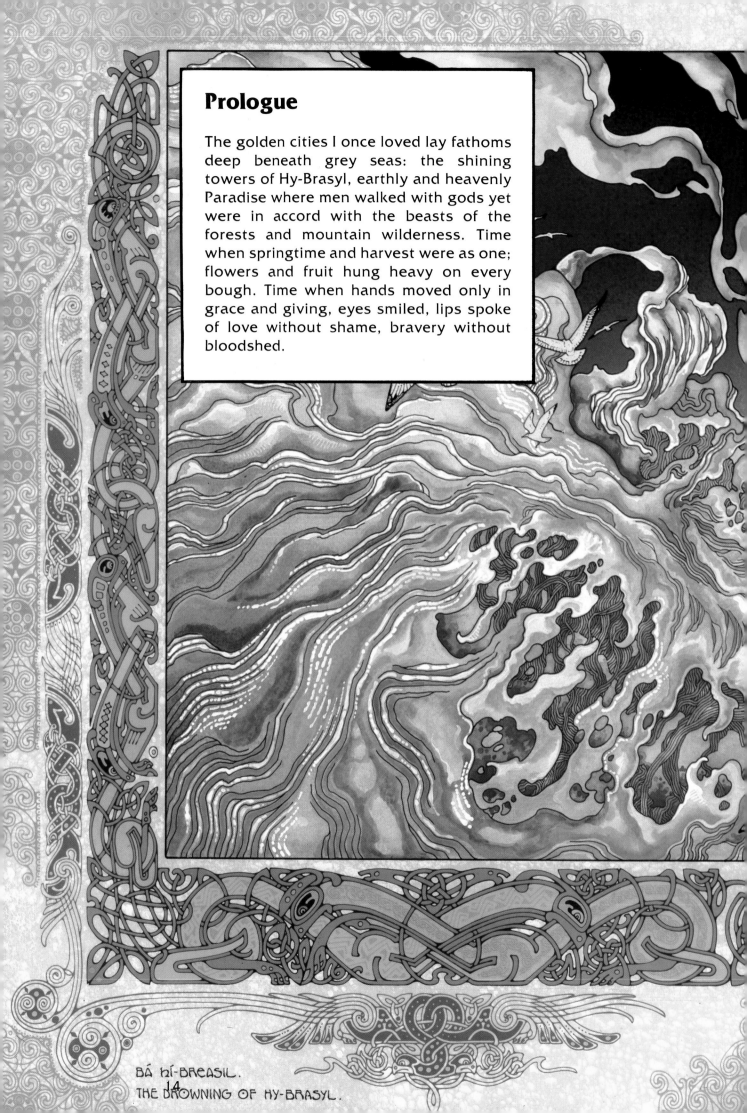

Prologue

The golden cities I once loved lay fathoms deep beneath grey seas: the shining towers of Hy-Brasyl, earthly and heavenly Paradise where men walked with gods yet were in accord with the beasts of the forests and mountain wilderness. Time when springtime and harvest were as one; flowers and fruit hung heavy on every bough. Time when hands moved only in grace and giving, eyes smiled, lips spoke of love without shame, bravery without bloodshed.

BÁ hí-BREASIL.
THE DROWNING OF HY-BRASYL.

FEABHRA·79
JIM FITZPATRICK

THE TRANSFORMATIONS OF TUAN

I am Tuan
I am legend
I am memory turned myth.

I am the story teller. Warriors and young boys creep away from the hearths of wine-halls to hear me. Greedy for tales of honour and history they watch my lips with bright eyes for I give them what is more precious than gold; treasure unlocked from my heart.

My words burn like flame in the darkness. I speak and hearts beat high, swords warm to the hand; under my spell boys become men.

But I know both the pain as well as the brightness of fire. I am the story teller who cannot find rest. The peace of death will never be mine. I am condemned to watch and to speak; my hand reaches in vain for the warrior's sword.

Once I, Tuan, was a man, the chieftain of a great race, the Cesair. My warriors sat on wolf skins; they raised golden goblets to me brimming with wine. Neither evil nor harm dared cross the threshold where I sat, my throne studded with jewels, inlaid with ivory.

At night young virgins unbuckled my leather corselet and unlaced my tunics of chequered silk. In the flickering light of torches my queen came to me naked. Together we lay on a couch of furs and her soft fingers traced the strength of my body, her touch made my face beautiful to me. I hid my eyes in the darkness of her hair, my blood pulsed high within me and I was as a careless youth again.

But the gods envy the happiness of men; flood and sword combined to destroy my people. Now the wine-hall stood empty, ruined; doorway and roof gaped wide to receive the beasts of the earth and the birds of the air. It was ordained that I alone should be saved to bear witness to my people's fate. I watched helpless while the fair land of Éireann was

TUAN THE GREAT STAG

LÚNASA ·79

TUAN AN FIA FIREANN MHÓR

JIM FITZPATRICK 17

ravaged by the scavengers and foes. The golden cities I once loved lay fathoms deep beneath grey seas.

For many years I wandered as a man seeking shelter in caves and the depths of the forest; but when at last the noble race of Nemed came to reclaim their homeland I was barred from greeting them as either chieftain or warrior. Another fate was mine; to watch unseen, keeping the secrets of time close in heart and brain. The gods had singled me out for a strange fate, unfamiliar pains and pleasures, for, as the years passed, they bound me within the bodies of beast and bird so that I might watch and keep the history of Éireann unnoticed by men.

The first transformation came upon me unaware. I had grown old as a man. The years had left my body naked and weak; my joints ached and my hair fell grey and matted over my bowed shoulders. One day a great weariness came upon me. I sought shelter in my cave certain that death had claimed me. For many days and nights I slept. Then at last I awoke to the sun. My limbs felt strong and free. My heart leapt up within me for I had been reborn as Tuan, the great-horned stag, King of the deer-herds of Éireann. The green hills were mine, the valleys and the streams.

As I ran free across the heather covered plains, the children of Nemed were driven from their homeland. Only I remained, grown old as a stag, their story locked in my heart. Then the great heaviness of change again weighed me down; again I sought shelter in my cave. Wolves eager for my blood and sinewy flesh howled to the moon. But I slept, floating loose in dream-time. Through the heaviness of sleep I felt myself grow young again. When the low rays of sunrise touched me I awoke.

The wolves still sniffed about the entrance to my cave. But now I was young and strong; fit to face them. I, Tuan, with joyful heart, thrust my sharp tusks out of my lair and the wolves fled yelping like frightened dogs. I was fresh, lusty with life; I had been born again, a black boar bristling with power, thirsty for blood. Now I was a king of herds; my back was sharp with dark bristles; my teeth and tusks were ready to cut and kill. All creatures feared me.

But while I had lain locked in dreams a new race of men had come to disturb the silence of mountain and valley. They were the Fir Bolg and they belonged to the family of Nemed. These I did not chase and when they chased me I fled, for their blood was mine also. The Fir Bolg divided the island into five provinces and proclaimed the title Ard-Rí, that is High King, for the first time in Éireann.

As I roamed the purple hills I would often leave my herd and gaze across to the High King's hall and remember with sadness the time when

I also had sat in council, with warriors at my feet, and felt the bright eyes of women gaze upon me.

Once again the ache of change drove me back to my lonely cave in Ulster. After three days fasting another death floated me beyond dream-time. Nights circled from summer into winter until one morning I woke and soared high into the clear sky.

I was reborn

I was lord of the heavens

I was Tuan the great sea-eagle.

I, who had been king among the heather and scented woodlands, became lord of the heavens. From the highest mountain I could see the field-mouse gathering wheat husks, nothing escaped my sharp eye.

Motionless, feathering the air, riding the wind, I watched the children of Nemed return to Éireann. Now known as the Tuatha Dé Danann they sailed down over the mountains in a magic fleet of sky riding ships until they came to rest among the Red Hills of Rein led by Nuada, their king.

Rather than fight their own flesh and blood the Tuatha Dé offered to share the island with the tribes of the Fir Bolg but on the advice of his elders Eochai, their High King, refused and the battle lines were drawn up.

I, Tuan the eagle, watched that fraticidal struggle; that terrible slaughter of kinsmen known as the First Battle of Moy Tura. I saw the same green plain across which I had, as a stag and boar, led my herd, drenched in blood. There I saw for the last time the Fir Bolg in their fullness and their pride, in their beauty and their youth, ranged against

MARTA 80

MOY TURA · THE PLAIN OF PILLARS
JIM FITZPATRICK 21

the glittering armies of the Tuatha Dé Danann. The battle was fierce and ebbed and flowed like waves on a sea of fortune and pride.

The circles of my eyes were rimmed with bitter tears as I watched that dreadful carnage of kinsmen, for all who fought were bound by a common bond, the blood of Nemed the Great. The battle raged for many days; death cut down the flower of the youth on both sides.

At last the Tuatha Dé Danann took the sovereignty of Éireann from the Fir Bolg and their allies. But in that First Battle of Moy Tura, Nuada, King of the Dé Dananns, had his arm struck off and from that loss there came sorrow and trouble to his people, for it was a law with the Tuatha Dé Danann that no man imperfect in form could be king. So it happened that Nuada who had led his people to victory had to abdicate his throne and hand the royal crown over to the elders of his race.

I, Tuan, the sea-eagle, wept secretly with Nuada over the loss of his crown, for he was a noble king and a just ruler who had won back the land of Éireann for his people. His mutilation and his loss were the result of his bravery in battle. For he was a great warrior, skilled and courageous and as one with his god, the Sun.

When the noise of battle and the wailing of women had faded into silence, when the earth had soaked up the blood, when the plain of Moy Tura had become a sad spirit-haunted place marked by pillars and cairns, I, Tuan, still sailed high above it. I knew that that same force of history that governed the fortunes of men had made me the winged bearer of myth. I knew that the pattern of change is never completed until the world's end. Still I would have to bear the burden of man's triumph and grief.

I am Tuan
I am Legend
I am memory turned myth.

I have lived through the ages
In the shape of man, beast and bird
Mute witness to great events,
Guardian of past deeds.

Now is the time
To tell another story:
The saga of Lugh, the Il-Dána;
Nuada of the Silver Arm
And the Second Battle of Moy Tura.

PART TWO

THE KINGSHIP OF BREAS

JIM FITZPATRICK

THE KINGSHIP OF BREAS

1. THE LIST OF FAME OF THE TUATHA DÉ DANANN

The law of the Gods forbade Nuada from being king because without his arm he was no longer whole in body. A new leader had to be chosen from the ranks of the Tuatha Dé Danann. Those who came after Nuada in rank, bravery and fame were:

Dagda, the All-Father, a god in human guise; big in body, bountiful in spirit he was the oldest and wisest of the Dé Danann chieftains.

Ogma, the brother of Dagda, to whom power of mind was greater than strength of sinew; he was both teacher and scholar, the first to spell out the Ogham script in which history is carved deep into the standing stones of Éireann.

After these brothers came Manannán Mac Lir, god of the sea, commander of the Dé Danann fleet. It was he who roamed the seas of the world with his magical air-born ships. He it was also who gave his name to the Isle of Man.

Then there was Breas the Beautiful, the son of Elathan, King of the Fomor. Reared among his mother's race, Breas was the greatest champion of the Tuatha Dé Danann. He proved his bravery beyond doubt at the First Battle of Moy Tura; but though beautiful and brave Breas was unforgiving and arrogant in his heart.

Others who lent their power to the victorious race were first the three-fold sisterhood of war witches, the Badb: Macha, Mórrigan and Nemain. They changed as the warriors' blood pulsed; one hour they were as beautiful as golden virgins but ready in a moment to harden into leathery harpies eager for blood and flesh.

Less terrible in their magic but as skillful in their own arts were:
Mórfhis the Druid, versed in ancient spells;
Dian-cécht the Healer, god of medicine;
Donn, ruler of the Dead, god of the Otherworld;
Goibhnu, Lúchta and Créidne the craftsman.

I, Tuan, watched them, unnoticed, as I wheeled a speck in the sky above their council on the hill of Tara, the Royal Seat. The Tuatha Dé had gathered there to choose their new king. I, alone, without vote or

BREAS AN ÁILLEACHT.
NOLLAG. 79

BREAS THE BEAUTIFUL
JIM FITZPATRICK

speech, knew that their choice would bring about fresh disaster and bloodshed.

Seduced by his beauty the women of the Tuatha Dé urged their men to elect Breas the Beautiful. They reasoned that his Fomor blood would seal the pact they had made on arrival by the marriage of Cian, son of Dian-Céht the healer and Balor's own daughter Eithne. Thus they might still rest safe from their hereditary enemy, the Fomor, led by their powerful wizard king, Balor of the Evil Eye. Such peace would leave them free to ally themselves with their erstwhile foes, the Fir Bolg, and at last rule Éireann in peace.

2. THE CONCEPTION OF BREAS AND THE VISION OF CARNÚN

So it came to pass that Breas the Beautiful stood ready to be crowned King of the Tuatha Dé Danann on the Hill of Hostages at Tara. Resplendent he stood alone on the sacred stone of destiny, Lia Fáil, while it roared beneath his feet as it would for all kings crowned in Éireann.

The day of his crowning was bright with promise for the Tuatha Dé. They saw no shadow but only their new king shining like hero and god, dressed in a bronze-plated ox-hide bodice. The warm wind filled his crimson, gold-embroidered cloak and lifted his blond hair which streamed like sunlight from beneath his ceremonial war-helmet, circled with sacred runic charms. His eyes were blue like sea and sky; his lips as finely tipped as arrow heads.

As Breas stood dressed in the colours of earth and sky, reflecting all the glory of the summer sun, he turned, as the custom was, to Ogma, the god of wisdom and learning and asked him to tell of his forebears so that he and his people should know from whence he came. So Ogma turned to Breas and before all his assembled people told him the story of his conception and birth. These were his words:

"One day Éri, daughter of a noble chieftain of the Tuatha Dé, stood gazing across the sea from her father's tower at Maeth Scéne. The water was as calm as a polished mirror but, as she watched, she saw a silver ship; driven by magical power it moved across the calm until at last it reached the shore beneath her window.

"At the prow of the ship stood a young man fairer than any other in her father's land. His hair was like a golden mane and his cloak and tunic were embroidered with shining thread; he carried two silver spears and his neck was circled by five rings of gold.

"As the ship grounded the golden prince leapt out and without hesitation climbed the spiral staircase to the room where Éri stood. Then this beautiful princess of the Tuatha Dé Danann, who had refused the love of all the bravest and most handsome men of her own land, felt her heart melt before the gaze of the fair stranger so that she lay with him and gave him her love.

"When he rose to go she wept. But the prince comforted her and taking his gold ring with its engravings of race and rank from his middle finger he placed it in her hand and closing his own hand over hers said:

"'You must never part with this ring except to one whose finger it shall fit. I am Elathan son of Delbaeth, King of the Fomor. After nine months you will bear a boy and he shall be called Breas which means beautiful.'

"Then the prince strode back to his silver ship and as Éri watched it glided across the calm sea until it vanished from her sight. And all came to pass as Elathan had foretold for after the appointed time Éri gave birth to a son whom she named Breas and he grew to be the strongest and most beautiful youth of the land.

"That," said Ogma the wise one, "is the story of Breas the Beautiful. I, Ogma, have kept this secret locked in my heart until this very day."

The people of the Tuatha Dé listened to Ogma's words and felt they had chosen wisely. Now had come the moment for them to pledge loyalty to their king. As the crown was placed on Breas's head the druid stone of Lia Fáil began to roar so loudly that the standing-stones of the Moy Tura plain wailed in awful unison. Awestruck the whole assembly of the tribe of Nemed fell to the ground in homage.

Only I, Tuan the sea-eagle, hovering high above them, saw the dark perspective of their future; how the Fir Bolg were not to forget the shame of their defeat at the First Battle of Moy Tura and how no man could trust the word of Balor or withstand the power of his Evil Eye.

While the Dé Dananns paid homage to their king I saw too what else was hidden from them: the ghostly shape of the terrible Horned God Carnún. In one hand he held a torc, a collar of rolled and twisted gold, in the other hand he held the writhing serpent-lord, Crom-Crúach. In a chill of fear I saw his great horns turn to flame and his eyes run red with blood.

As quickly as it had appeared the spectre vanished. Then I saw I was not the sole witness of this horror; far below me the upturned face of Breas was whiter than snow, paler than death. He too had seen the sign and knew that his reign was to be cursed with bloodshed and disaster.

ERI AND THE SON OF
THE KING OF THE FOMOR
28
ERI AGUS MAC RÍ NA bhFOMOR.

3. THE RULE OF BREAS THE BEAUTIFUL

True to the omen, the reign of Breas was cursed from the beginning. But the force of evil may wound, not vanquish, a brave and generous man. So it was that the curse came from the emptiness of the new king's heart and spirit, for the shape of the future and the destinies of heroes are fashioned by their choices for good or ill. Death cannot erase the name of a great man from the true story I tell, the feats of the brave last longer in words from the heart than if they were inscribed on pillars of gold.

In spite of his beauty and bravery, Breas was no leader of men and he brought dark times upon his people. Unable to resist the demands of his father's race, the Fomor, and terrified of their leader, Balor of the Evil Eye, Breas indulged their greed for taxes and tributes in exchange for peace.

It was true that the Tuatha Dé, weakened by the First Battle of Moy Tura were in no state to re-engage in war, but now their lives became no more than a dishonoured living death. Even the hearths and fires of Breas's people were taxed, also their cows and the milk they gave. In desperation they turned to tricks and strategems, but in vain, and so gradually they grew weaker in body and spirit.

Even the champions of Breas's court suffered hardship and humiliation, for their king lacked in generosity and courtesy. The heroes' knives went ungreased and their horn cups were never filled with ale. Neither was there merriment nor pleasure in the palace; no call for the singers or harpers, for poets and bards, fools or jugglers, so the very history of the people was left unspoken and unsung. The great festivals were left unobserved and the trials of champions lapsed. The only use for strength and spirit was when it was put to work for the king. Heroes and wisemen alike became no more than slaves.

Ogma, god of wisdom and glorious poet, was made to bring firewood to the Royal Palace. Every day he would bring a bundle from the shore, but soon he became so weak from lack of food that the sea would sweep two-thirds of his wood away and his debt to Breas grew until it burdened him almost to death.

Dagda, the All-Father, once god and provider of his people, fell into disgrace with the king, for Breas had set him to build the Royal Fortress. But Dagda's appetite was great and his master gave him no more food than would keep a sparrow-hawk alive and favoured an idle flatterer, a sharp tongued blind man called Cidínbél, more than the hero and god of his people. Each night Cidínbél would say:

"For the sake of your good name and honour let the three best bits be given to me, O Dagda."

Dagda would not dishonour himself by refusing, so he passed his portion to the blind man. Thus gradually Dagda grew weaker, until one day his son Aengus came upon his father as he was labouring to strengthen the Fortress of Breas. Aengus was shocked by his father's wretchedness and when he had learned the cause he said to the Dagda:

"Take these three pieces of gold and put them in the three best portions of your food tonight."

So Dagda did as Aengus said and when Cidínbél demanded and received the hero's portion from Dagda's plate, he ate and fell dead. Breas and his supporters cried out that the Dagda had poisoned the blind man, but the god and hero of the Tuatha Dé said:

"Your judgement is unworthy of a king of our race." And then he went on to tell what had happened each night in the hall and how at last he had given the three best portions, gold and all, to Cidínbél. The king ordered the body of the blind man to be cut open and the gold was discovered, so it was proved that the Dagda spoke truly and King Breas was further dishonoured among his own people.

4. THE DELIRIUM OF NUADA

While Breas the Beautiful ruled from the throne of Tara, Nuada lay in his tent tormented by sickness of body and mind. For while the loss of his three sons at the First Battle of Moy Tura grieved him and his mutilated arm caused him sore pain, it was the loss of his king-ship that was the greatest shame and agony to him.

He had spent his life planning for the day when he would bring his people back to the promised homeland of Éireann. He had kept that promise; he had conquered their enemies; he had won them the right to live in peace, but now his people had turned from him and looked to Breas for leadership, a man unworthy to be king, who bent their laws to suit himself and meet the insatiable demands of the Fomor.

Now a fever seized Nuada, and as his mind twisted and turned under its spell he saw himself as though swept back to the beginning of time. First there was only the dark void; then it was pierced with stars. In his delirium Nuada saw the earth as it was when first made and the creator of men moved among his children, the race of Nemed, in the fresh richness of the world he had fashioned for them. Great green-scaled reptiles moved against towering forests of ferns and curtains of moss; bronze skinned dragons dwelt in glittering palaces hollowed from white quartz mountains that towered against purple skies. But as Nuada moved through time the palaces crumbled; floods destroyed the gardens of the earth, and the great and gentle creatures were slaughtered by a dark and evil race of men: the Fomor led by the wizard lord Balor of the Evil Eye and his war-chieftain Conánn the Conqueror. Then Nuada witnessed the disasters and triumphs of his own people and their arrival at the promised land of Éireann.

And so it came that Nuada's dreams were tormented with memories of that Battle of Moy Tura where he had received his grievous wound and lost his crown. He saw the flower of his warriors fall beneath the scythe of Death; he felt again the power of those indifferent Fates, who cut the threads of men's destinies without reason or pity. The Pillars of the battlefield of Moy Tura revolved around him showing long perspectives of death, the cairns of the dead, women weeping for husbands, sons and fathers.

In the agony of his delirium Nuada called on Morrígan, war-witch possessed of terrible beauty, to comfort him in his dark and painful dreaming.

High up in my eyrie, I, the sea-eagle Tuan, saw a huge raven plummet down on the tent of Nuada. As it alighted on a tight-drawn hawser it spread out its wings, silver-blue in the moonlight, and I knew it for what it was. I watched it change into a woman, her pale nakedness shrouded by dark hair. It was Morrígan, the crow of battle, also beautiful war-witch, who had come to answer the anguished call of Nuada. As she entered Nuada's tent my heart ached, for I remembered the time when I too was a king and received pleasure and comfort from that same dark-haired woman who was my queen, but now lost to me forever.

PART THREE

THE RE-INSTATEMENT OF NUADA OF THE SILVER ARM

THE RE-INSTATEMENT OF NUADA OF THE SILVER ARM

1. THE CURES OF MIACH

While Mórrigan comforted Nuada in his agony of spirit, Dian-cécht the Healer, tended his stricken arm, sealing the terrible wound with a secret mixture of burnt herbs and rushes.

But Dian-cécht had a son called Miach, who set himself in rivalry against his father's old ways of healing. During the First Battle of Moy Tura a young warrior had lost his eye through a spear thrust and he came to Miach for a cure, so famous were the young man's magical powers.

The young warrior said to Miach:

"If you are as good a healer as I have heard tell, give me an eye in place of the one I have lost."

"I could put the eye of that cat on your lap in its place," answered Miach.

And Miach did what he said and the hero went away happy in the fullness of his sight. But afterwards it was said that he would have been better without such healing because at night, when he tried to sleep, his cat's eye would blink open in the dark at the sound of mice squeaking, or creatures in the rushes, and in the day, when he was eager to watch a trial of strength or a pretty girl, the eye was sure to be sound asleep.

Miach was contemptuous of his father's healing of Nuada's arm, for the king was still not whole, but without sword hand or forearm. So the young healer took the decayed hand that had been struck off and whispered spells over it:

'Limb to limb and sinew to sinew
Thus shall the cure be made.'

Miach stayed twenty-seven days with Nuada; the first nine days he placed the arm against the hero's side; the second nine days he placed it against his breast and it covered itself with skin; the third nine days he poulticed it with fire-blackened bullrushes and after all this the arm was secured and healed.

His son's success did not please Dian-cécht. He accused Miach of evil sorcery and swore that he would bring down the wrath of the gods on the people of the Tuatha Dé. In anger he hurled his sword at his son's head; three times he struck him, each time Miach healed his own wound,

MÓRRIGAN NA BADB

MÓRRIGAN OF THE BADB.

SAMHAIN ·79

JIM FITZPATRICK 35

but on the fourth time his father broke open his skull, so that his brains burst forth and even Miach could not repair that hurt.

So Dian-cécht, the father, buried Miach his son and rival in healing. Yet even in death Miach's powers survived and three-hundred and sixty-five herbs, matching the number of his joints and sinews, grew up from his grave. Airmed, his sister, came to the grave of Miach one day and spreading her blue-grey cloak on the ground, laid out the herbs according to their virtues and properties. But when Dian-cécht saw this, he threw her cloak into the air and mixed up all the herbs, so that no man to this day knows their properties.

2. NUADA'S JOURNEY TO THE OTHER WORLD

While Nuada lay close to death, the Badb came to him: Macha, the goddess of war; Nemhain, the goddess of battle-frenzy and Mórrigan, the raven queen. The three war-witches lit a wax taper and smeared their bodies with black ash, white chalk and the juice of the red berry. As Nuada tossed in pain they chanted their spells:

" God of darkness
Lord of death
Ruler of shadows
Hear us.

In thunder, lightning
Flood or fire
We await you.

We are the three sisters
Battle harpies, phantom queens
An unholy trinity, the Badb.

We put our bodies
Between you and Nuada;
Between the Lord of Death
And a child of the sun.

Empty your heart of the want of this hero
The desire for his soul.

Turn his face away from death
Spare him for life.

God of darkness
Lord of death
Ruler of shadows
Hear us."

While the Badb prayed to the God of Death, Dian-cécht, master of healing, summoned his own spirits to help him cure Nuada, his beloved king.

Late that same night Donn, Ruler of the Dead among the Tuatha Dé Danann, came to the royal tent and joined the Badb in their spells and charms. He covered the body of Nuada, now still as death, with white chalk and limed the hero's hair until it was stiff and hard as a boar's bristled back. Then Donn dipped his finger in a bowl of soft blue woad and inscribed protective runes on the cold, white body of Nuada. Then he sent forth the king's soul on a journey out of time and life, in the hope that Nuada himself would find the cure for his sickness of body and mind, strength against death.

For three days and three nights Nuada lay in a trance; often the hard white chalk softened and ran wet with his secret pain.

I, Tuan, followed Nuada in his black dreams. He walked across the dark fields of night, stepping among stars until his way was barred by a huge flame, brighter than a hundred suns, rayed with tentacles of red smoke. The fire parted to show a path leading to an even more dreadful darkness. At its end Nuada saw two eyes, ice-cold and cruel. Then, across those far reaches of time and space, echoed a disembodied cry, the eyes dimmed and Nuada was left alone in the black void. As the voice continued to speak, Nuada saw a great mouth before him, twisting with mocking words:

"Nuada you have come
To a world without pain
And without pleasure;
Return now and pain not
Pleasure awaits you.
Once whole, you are now less,
Less for the loss of an arm
And a kingdom."

JIM FITZPATRICK

Nuada drew his Sword of Light, the magical Claimh Solais, from its scabbard and tried to still the mouth that taunted him. But even as he lunged forward the mouth roared with such power of defiance and derision that Nuada was blown backwards, and the Sword of Light wrenched from his hands and sent wheeling away into the dark wasteland of eternal night.

Falling away through time, Nuada found himself again on some forgotten earth, both strange and familiar. He seemed to stand in the centre of a huge plateau drained of colour, caught in perpetual twilight. The ground was rough with curiously piled cairns and burial mounds, but above these rose line upon line of standing stones and monoliths, some graven with the Ogham script, some untouched by craftsman's art and others beautifully wrought and richly engraved. They stood, lonely sentinels, ranged across the plain of death.

Nuada turned and saw another battle-plain, but different from the first, for the Battle Pillars stood uneven and at random, some tall and others twisted and eroded. Ancient and marked with obscure lichen covered words and carvings, broken and precariously balanced, these stones spelt out another, older, age of evil and unnatural practices.

Then invisible hands lifted Nuada away from these plains of pillars and bore him to a grey hill. On the hill stood a great palace. Whirlwinds raged about it and he heard faraway voices wailing in anguish, calling out words that he could not understand. He walked to the gates of the palace and stood before them in the half light while stars drifted at his feet.

As he stood, the myriad lights clustered round him and he saw the Sword of Light. He reached out for it and it came to his bidding, but as he did so he saw that he grasped it not with his good right arm but with his hacked, decaying limb, a hand that was a shapeless mass of rotten flesh seething with stub-headed maggots. Nuada recoiled with horror from his own wound, sign of his mortality and death.

In a rage of fury and disgust he bade the magic sword to strike his rotting arm from his body and so it did, though he felt no pain. As his death fell away so the stars gathered around him and cloaked him in the cold magnificence of their fire.

Thus Nuada stood stripped naked and helpless as a child, bathed in starlight. Then each point of light gathered and massed quivering with strange life around Nuada's shattered arm. The elements of earth, water, wind, fire and ice mixed to make a crystalline sand out of the starfire. As the hero watched he saw a new limb forged from light, an arm of purest silver into which a beam of crimson flame sank, making it pulse with a mysterious life-force. Then a flash of blue lightning coiled round his body and fused the silver arm to his flesh in a burst of radiant energy.

The cloak of starlight fell away and Nuada found himself standing once more before the gates of the great palace. His was the arm of silver, his was the Sword of Light. The doors of the palace opened. Nuada was whole again and glad of heart.

NUADA JOURNEYS
TO THE
OTHERWORLD

TURAS NUADA 3⁰ DOMHAN SAOLEILE

JIM FITZPATRICK

3. NUADA OF THE SILVER ARM

At last Nuada woke from his dream, dazed and uncomprehending. Around him the wax tapers flickered and the ash-smeared faces of the beautiful war-goddesses, the Badb, gazed down at him. Donn, ruler of the dead, towered above him and Dian-cécht, the healer leant over him.

Nuada looked down at his naked body, covered in damp smears of chalk and woad, and he saw that his dream had become truth, for instead of a withered stump he had indeed a new arm of purest silver. It fitted his arm as a glove fits a hand and had movement in every joint and sinew. It was engraved with interlocking spirals that shimmered with unnatural life in the fitful light of the tapers. Across the silver hand the runes of his race and rank were etched, tightening into a triple band around his wrist.

Nuada knew it was a hand forged by gods, not men, and so he rose from his sickbed and clasped his silver fingers around the hilt of the Sword of Light. Slowly he drew it from its scabbard and, lifting the flap of his tent, he stepped out into the morning mists. He felt the warmth of the sacred soil of Éireann beneath his feet and it was good. He raised his magic sword to the rising sun and his battle-cry echoed across the hills of Royal Tara for the first time after many years of silence.

"Lámh Láidir Abú," he cried to the echoing hills. "Lámh Láidir Abú," they answered.

"I am Nuada, son of the Sun
I am he of the Silver-Arm"

From that day that was his name, and even today the people of Éireann speak in awe of Nuada Airged Lámh, that is Nuada of the Silver Arm.

During those three nights and days while Nuada hung close to death, I, Tuan, keeper of this tale, had kept close watch on Tara's hills and shared the King's pain.

Now, as I heard his war-cry echoing through the morning mists, I rejoiced, and rode the high gold of the dawn clouds and gave thanks to the rising sun.

4. THE REINSTATEMENT OF NUADA

One day in summer, a poet of the Tuatha Dé, Cairbre, son of Étain, came to the court of King Breas; he was given scant welcome and not even drink to quench his thirst. In return he wrote the Royal Blessing backwards so that it spelt the end of Breas's rule.

From that day onwards Breas lost his power and the allegiance of his people. No one paid taxes and all the warriors and tribes of the Tuatha Dé demanded the reinstatement of their previous King, Nuada of the Silver Arm, now made magically whole again. They sent word to Breas, asking him to return both crown and realm. Breas agreed to give up the crown and the lands, but begged that he might be allowed to remain in the kingship until the end of his seventh year, so that he would not be rendered destitute.

"That shall be granted," said Nuada. "For you served us well as champion and warrior, and though your reign has been an unfortunate one, we still think of your deeds on the battlefield of Moy Tura and how you turned the battle in our favour time and time again. But you must cease levying taxes on our people and end your allegiance to Balor of the Evil Eye."

"I will do as you ask," answered Breas. Nuada and his elders knew that they would incur the wrath of Balor and the Fomor tribes, and so, the year and a half that followed, Nuada spent in reforming his battalions and training his young warriors. Those veterans who remained from the First Battle of Moy Tura were put in charge of each war-group.

The fair Dé Danann warriors marched across the plains of Tara. The earth resounded; wild creatures hid from their battle cries, the glitter and tumult of tribe after tribe. Women and children took delight in the spectacle, forgetting the bloodshed it boded.

Because he had few seasoned warriors left from the First Battle of Moy Tura, Nuada had to display his forces as best he could. Battle strategy had to take the place of hand to hand fighting and the trials of heroes. Nuada knew that the Fomor were fierce and passionate fighters who swept all before them with the violence of their onslaught, the fear roused by their war cries and the unearthly aspect of their battle paint. This very wildness, which had served them so well in the past, might lead to their downfall if met by a solid front of warriors trained to fight together in tightly disciplined battle formations.

If the savage Fomor warriors could be separated and trapped by the Dé Danann forces they would fall easy prey to weapons wielded with cool intelligence and foresight. The spells of the druids and the power of their gods would serve to strengthen the stratagems and arms of the Tuatha Dé and make them well nigh invincible.

Nuada's plan was this: that each battalion of men should present a solid wall of shields bristling with spears; each warrior standing firm with his neighbour. To the left and right of the vanguard, as if completing the sides of a square, would stand another row of men, their shield wall turned outwards. These men, bearing long shields and spears, would also be protecting a battle partner who carried a sword and dagger; on the right and left flank there would be two shield carriers to every skilled swordsmen, chosen from those seasoned warriors who had escaped the carnage of the First Battle of Moy Tura; men cunning and experienced in fighting and unafraid of the terrible din and war cries of the enemy.

Nuada knew that the Fomor were used to scything down an enemy numb with terror at the wild ferocity and battle frenzy that made each man seem a supernatural being, a devil sent from the realms of evil; so he instructed each battalion to hold firm against men who were neither gods nor devils but mere savages. The solid wall of shields was to remain firm until the first Fomor warriors were impaled on the palisade of spears, only then was the front line of the Tuatha Dé to retreat, still holding firm shoulder to shoulder. As the Fomor followed them so the right and left flanks of each Dé Danann battalion would advance and close together, forming a triangular space in which the Fomor would be trapped. Then every other shield bearer would turn, and cover his swordsman waiting ready behind him, while he dealt out mortal wounds to the tight-packed enemy caught in a confusion made all the greater because of the sudden halt of their frenzied battle-charge. The shield bearers had to remain firm, shoulder to shoulder, trusting their partners to protect them from behind while they in turn held off others of the advancing enemy force.

Again and again the men of the Tuatha Dé performed their battle drill, until they responded as a single body to the commands of their leaders. As he watched his army with pride, Nuada turned to Dagda and said:

"If Balor and his Fomor savages were here now to see our warriors train, they would think twice before demanding further tribute from us." Then with a mighty war-cry Nuada of the Silver Arm threw the Sword of Light high above him in the evening air; for a moment it hung in the air above him, catching the last rays of the setting sun and sending long beams of gold across the dappled plain of Royal Tara.

I, Tuan the great sea-eagle, hung high over Tara that summer's day and saw the tightly knit battalions of the warriors of the Tuatha Dé and shared in the exhultation of the hero-king restored to them again: Nuada of the Silver Arm.

BREAS AGUS CÚ BREA

BREAS AND CÚ BREA

JIM FITZPATRICK

45

In the shadow of my wings
I shelter the children of Nemed;
Their beauty I praise,
Their grace I celebrate,
Their valour I encourage,
Their pride I share.

5. BREAS JOURNEYS TO THE LAND OF THE FOMOR

Breas was vexed and dispirited by the turn of events, so he went to his mother, Éri. She gave him the golden ring that his father Elathan had put in her hand, all those years before, when he had come to her in the magic silver ship.

Éri advised Breas to gather about him a band of loyal men and to sail across the cold seas with her to those mist-shrouded islands where his father's people lived, the savage Fomor.

Breas did as his mother bade him and landed on that far distant shore under a flag of truce. Men of the Fomor tribe led Breas, Éri and their followers to the great camp of Indech, son of the chieftain of the Northern Fomor, and Elathan, the Immortal, Breas's father and sea-lord of the Fomor.

Neither Breas nor his mother claimed kinship with Elathan. They and their followers came as people of Éireann and as was the custom when warriors of different tribes met peaceably, they were challenged to a friendly contest, in this case a dog race, which served to divert the passions of young warriors otherwise eager for real battle and bloodshed.

6. THE GREAT DOG-RACE

The preparations for the dog-race lasted well into the night and gave the Fomor opportunity to impress their visitors with their vast battle array, for lines of Fomor warriors in full armour marked out the circular course of the race.

Breas's favourite hound, Cú Brea, dozed beside his master's tent; the other dogs of Éireann sniffed idly around. When dawn came they stretched themselves and went down to join their Fomor rivals, who backed away, snarling, from such formidable opponents.

Breas stroked Cú Brea's neck and from his master's touch the hound gathered a hero's strength to add to his own competitive spirit.

A great roar went up as the dogs were unleashed. Immediately Cú Brea took the lead and sped across the silver dew of morning. Through bracken and heather he ran until he came to a rushing stream; without hesitation he plunged into it and easily climbed its slippery bank. But when he came to the top of the neighbouring hill, one of the Fomor warriors reached out and kicked him. Cú Brea lost his footing and slipped back. As he regained his balance the same foot came out and kicked him again.

This time the enraged hound flew at the throat of his tormentor and tore it open. The Fomor warriors fled terrified, for the bite of a mad dog meant death. The race continued but now both packs were full of blood lust. As Breas watched anxiously, Cú Brea came into sight; he had won the race and those who came second and third were also dogs of Éireann.

Then the champions of Fomor challenged the strangers to a contest of battle skills. Seven times Breas fought and won; at last Elathan himself stepped forward and challenged the victorious stranger, but when Breas lifted his sword the chieftain recognised the ring he had given to his mistress, Éri. Immediately Elathan embraced the young hero saying:

"You are my son, for no other can have the name Breas and wear this ring."

"I am indeed your son," replied Breas. Then they wept in each other's arms and Éri joined them.

During that night's feasting Breas told his father that he had come to seek support to win back his crown. But after Elathan had questioned him Breas was forced to admit that he had ruled unwisely, with greed, injustice and arrogance. Though a Fomor, Elathan was an honourable man and he rebuked his son, saying:

"I cannot help you to regain a crown that you dishonoured. You must go and ask the advice of our Wizard Lord, Balor of the Strong Blows."

7. THE MEETING OF BREAS THE BEAUTIFUL WITH BALOR OF THE EVIL EYE.

And so Breas, escorted by his father's men, followed a dark river to its source deep in the heart of the forest. The water sprang from cupped hands carved out of basalt. No sunlight penetrated the gloom, but strange mists and vapours coiled and twisted out of the black spray of the water so that nothing seemed certain; even the ground at Breas's feet seemed to melt away into deep chasms echoing with the cries of a thousand grief-stricken souls.

The hero's heart and hands were cold with fear. His Fomor escort led Breas forward and as the mists parted before them he saw a palace of ebony, the solid heart of darkness. This was the house of Balor, he who was older than the world itself, he who could stop the hearts of men by opening his single eye or with a single flashing glance reduce a host to ashes.

Breas, his hand tight on his sword hilt, entered the great hall. Here the darkness seemed to quiver with unnatural life. Galleries and broken staircases ran along the high walls; obscene carvings writhed up pillars, framed empty doorways, or were lost or hidden behind tapestries which seemed to veil unspeakable monstrosities, or heave with a terrifying life of their own.

In the centre of the hall there was set an orb of crystal, pulsing with glowing light. Breas felt its force engulf him, drawing him ever nearer.

"You gaze upon the threshold of the Otherworld, Breas son of Elathan."

The voice echoed round the hall becoming one with the shifting shadows.

"Who speaks?" asked Breas.

"Balor of the Strong Blows speaks to you son of the Fomor," said the voice, and the shadows joined to clothe a huge figure without face or limbs.

"You wish to regain your lost honour and be avenged against the Tuatha Dé Danann?" asked Balor.

"I do," said Breas.

"Then I will help you," said Balor. The wizard raised two long grey hands to where his head should be. First, two yellow eyes blinked open, and then, above and between them, grew a silver disc on which a third eye was engraved, but shut. Then Balor passed a polished handle through the disc and the silver eye opened and sent forth a beam of light which was absorbed by the pulsing crystal orb. Then the lid of the eye closed again and images began to form in the crystal.

As Balor and Breas watched, they saw first the Hill of Uisneach near Tara, then they saw a foreshadowing of the events which were to determine the life of one, and the death of the other, at the Second Battle of Moy Tura.

PART FOUR

THE COMING OF THE IL-DÁNA

THE COMING OF THE IL-DÁNA

1. THE COMING OF LUGH TO UISNEACH.

This was the vision that Breas and Balor saw unfolded in the crystal:

The Hill of Uisneach was covered with the tents and fluttering banners of the Fair-Meeting of Nuada of the Silver Arm. When Nuada announced the abolition of the Fomor taxes there was great celebration among his people.

Then, at the height of their festivities, the Tuatha Dé saw a band of warriors riding over the crest of the hill. They were all mounted on white horses and led by the fairest and most handsome of men.

Thus came Lugh Lamh-Fada, the Il-Dána, riding his great white horse Aonvarr of the Flowing Mane; no one seated on her could fall or be killed. He wore Manannan's coat of twice smelted chain mail which no sword could pierce. His horned helmet had two glittering stones set in front and one behind. At his side hung his sword, Freagra, the Answerer; no man could survive a wound from it. Lugh had come with his foster brothers, sons of the sea god Manannan Mac Lir, and they headed a band of warriors who belonged to the Shí, the Faerie host, Riders in the Sky.

"This is a magic troop," said Dagda. And Nuada admitted that he had never seen the like of such a hero before.

Lugh, the Il-Dána, was the Man of Sciences and Many Talents. He was the grandson of Balor of the Evil Eye himself, offspring of the union of Balor's daughter, Ethne and Cian, son of Dian-cécht, the Dé Danann Healer, and his foster-mother had been Tailltu, queen of the Fir Bolg. All the races of Éireann were mingled in his blood; in his life and history Lugh was to be counted legendary among heroes.

2. THE WRATH OF THE IL-DÁNA.

Thus Lugh, destined to be the greatest hero of the Tuatha Dé Danann, came to his king, Nuada of the Silver Arm.

THE COMING OF LÚGH
THE IL-DÁNA
MEÁN FÓMHAIR · 79

TEACHT LÚGH SAMIL·DANACH
JIM FITZPATRIC 51

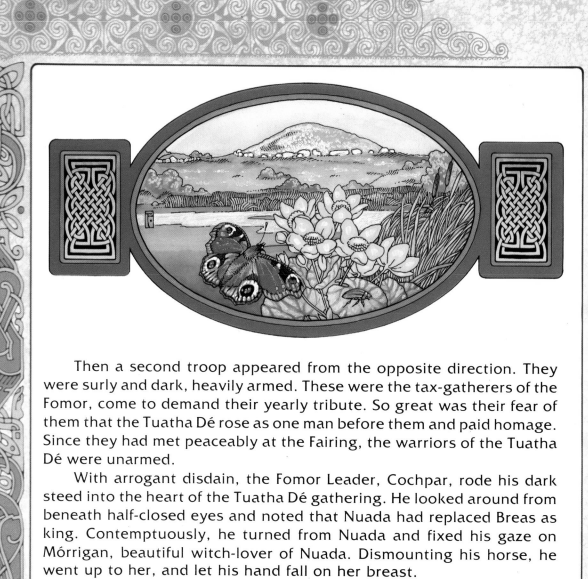

Then a second troop appeared from the opposite direction. They were surly and dark, heavily armed. These were the tax-gatherers of the Fomor, come to demand their yearly tribute. So great was their fear of them that the Tuatha Dé rose as one man before them and paid homage. Since they had met peaceably at the Fairing, the warriors of the Tuatha Dé were unarmed.

With arrogant disdain, the Fomor Leader, Cochpar, rode his dark steed into the heart of the Tuatha Dé gathering. He looked around from beneath half-closed eyes and noted that Nuada had replaced Breas as king. Contemptuously, he turned from Nuada and fixed his gaze on Mórrigan, beautiful witch-lover of Nuada. Dismounting his horse, he went up to her, and let his hand fall on her breast.

Lugh turned to Nuada and asked:

"Why do you let yourself be dishonoured thus?"

"For the moment we are not strong enough to do otherwise," said the king. "At the slightest protest they could kill us all."

When Lugh heard this he brooded in silence for a while and then he said:

"By the gods I feel a great desire to kill these savages."

But still Nuada and his tribe stood silently before the Fomor.

Then Lugh spoke again:

"By the Gods I will kill them myself then!"

"If you do," said the king, "it will only bring us worse evil, for the Fomor will send their forces before we are fully prepared."

But Lugh's blood ran cold as an icy stream and his steel-blue eyes glazed with anger. He turned to his Fairie Host and mounting Aonvarr

cried to the silent assembly of the Tuatha Dé:

"This dishonour has lasted long enough!" Drawing his magic sword he charged the Fomor chieftain and struck his head from his shoulders. Lugh's followers came after their prince and slaughtered the rest of the Fomor Tax Gatherers, all except nine. These he spared because they ran and put themselves under the protection of Nuada.

Then Lugh put his sword back into its scabbard and said:

"I would slay you also except that I wish you to go back to the land of the Fomor and tell the Wizard Lord, Balor, what you have seen here today."

3. THE PROPHECY OF CATHLEANN.

Balor needed no messenger to report that day's events; all was caught within the crystal globe deep in the heart of his black palace. Both he and Breas had seen the coming of the Il-Dána, though they did not know of his origin.

Then Balor summoned his wife, Cathleann, the prophetess. He showed her the image of the fair hero in his magical eye-pendant.

Cathleann paled and turned from the vision of the young hero.

"You know this youth?" asked Balor.

"I do," said Cathleann "and it would have been better for us if we had never seen him." She was silent awhile and then spoke again:

"He is your own grandson, born of the Tuatha Dé. He is almighty, all-powerful, invincible. His coming has been long foretold and it spells the

end of our own power in Éireann, even the end of your own life, O Balor of the Strong Blows, King of the Fomor.

"He is Lugh, the Il-Dána, the master of all sciences; his coming is our doom."

"It is true that it is prophesied that I will die by the hand of my own grandson," said Balor, "but this cannot be he, for, when my daughter Eithne gave birth to the child of Cian, the baby was drowned under my strictest orders. It will take more than this hero to destroy our ancient empire."

Then Balor, Breas, Cathleann and all the druids and sorcerers of the Fomor gathered in council with Balor's twelve sons. At last Breas the Beautiful spoke:

"I will go to Éireann with seven of the strongest Fomor battalions and find this Il-Dána and bring his head back and cast it at your feet."

The council agreed to Breas's plan and set to preparing warships and provisions for Breas and his army.

Messengers were sent to summon the strongest warriors and most skilful horsemen.

When they were assembled in full battle-array they looked invincible; an army of Gods.

Laughing, Balor turned to Breas and said:

"Bring me the head of the Il-Dána and then tie the island of Éireann to your ships and let the dark waters fill its place. Bring it to the north of this land where no Dé Danann will ever follow it."

Then, hoisting their sails, they loosed their moorings and sailed across the dark sea to the green land of Éireann.

As they disappeared beyond the horizon, Balor turned to his battle-commander, Indech, and said:

"Let Breas and his fleet serve to distract the army of the Tuatha Dé Danann and draw the power of the Il-Dána and I will secretly return to the

BALOR OF THE EVIL EYE

BALOR BIRUZDERC.

far shore of Éireann and put an end once and for all to the power of these arrogant tribes."

4. THE IL-DÁNA ENTERS ROYAL TARA

With the Fair of Uisneach ended, Nuada and his assembly went to Tara to prepare for the war they knew must follow the killing of the Fomor tax-gatherers.

Lugh and his troop followed soon after. He strode up to the palace gates and bade the doorkeeper to take him to the king. But the doorkeeper did not recognise either the hero or his name; so he called on the Il-Dána to identify himself and name his skills. For each of the skills that Lugh named there was already a practiced master within the palace; but at last Lugh told the doorkeeper to go and ask Nuada if he knew of any one man who possessed all these arts.

When Nuada heard of Lugh's coming he said:

"Let him come in, for never before has his like entered this fortress."

The doorkeeper returned to Lugh and, curious, asked him which arts he counted as the greatest. And Lugh replied:

"Swimming forever without tiring,

Carrying a vat between my elbows,

Outrunning the swiftest of horses,

Leaping on a bubble without breaking it."

Then the doorkeeper bade him welcome, and would have unbarred the gates, but Lugh prevented him saying:

"Do not open the gates now for the sun has set and it is unlucky to unlock them till dawn."

Then Lugh gathered his muscles together like a mountain wild-cat and with one great leap cleared the fortress wall of the Hosting Hall at Royal Tara and took his place among the warriors of the Tuatha Dé Danann.

I, Tuan, rejoiced in his coming. There was only one man who could rescue the children of Nemed from bondage and humiliation and that man, Lugh the Il-Dána, had come.

PART FIVE

THE
TRACK OF THE
DAGDA'S CLUB

THE TRACK OF THE DAGDA'S CLUB

1. THE ROLL-CALL OF POWER

When Nuada of the Silver Arm heard of Lugh's skills and arts he looked closely at the young man:

"You are well named, Lugh Samil-Dánach. I believe that you will indeed help us free ourselves from the Fomor tyrants."

Then Nuada stepped down from his throne and put Lugh in his place. For thirteen days the King, his nobles and his wise men, listened to the advice of the young hero.

First Lugh asked Mórfhis the druid what he could do:

"The twelve chief mountains of Éireann will roll their summits against the ground at my bidding."

Then Lugh asked the cup-bearers what they could give:

"We will put an unquenchable thirst upon the Fomor armies, but the twelve great lakes and the twelve great rivers of Éireann will be hidden from their sight, so that only the true men of Éireann will find water."

Figol, son of Mamós, the wizard, spoke next:

"I will cause three showers of fire to fall on the Fomor and I will seal their own urine and that of their horses within their bodies, so that poison will stagnate in their blood. I will also double every breath that the men of Éireann take, so their valor and strength will be multiplied seven-fold."

Lugh turned next to the Badb, the three war goddesses:

"We will enchant the trees, the stones, the very grains of the soil, so that at our bidding the earth itself will turn upside down beneath the feet of the Fomor."

Then Lugh asked Goibhnu, the smith, what power he could bring:

"Though the men of Éireann fight for seven years, I will renew every blade and spearhead that shatters in battle. No spear point cast by my hand ever misses its mark."

"And you, Créidne," said Lugh to his craftsman:

"Rivets for spears, hilts for swords, bosses and rims for shields; I shall supply them all."

Lugh turned to his carpenter Lúchta:

"I will give our army all that they need of stout shields and strong spear shafts."

When Lugh turned to Ogma, the God of Knowledge said:

"I will repel Indech and three-times nine of his army so that the men of Éireann will capture one-third of his army."

"And you Mórrigan" said Lugh "what power will you lend us?"

"Easy to say," said the beautiful war goddess, "I will strike their manhood; what I cut will never again be made whole."

Then Lugh questioned Dian-cécht, god of healing:

"However badly a man be hurt, unless his head be severed, by the morrow I will make him whole again!"

At last Lugh turned to Cairbre, son of Étain the poet of the Tuatha Dé:

"I will compose a satire, an oath song," said Cairbre. "And at sunrise on the day of battle, with a stone in one hand and a thorn in the other, I will sing this poem to bring shame within the heart and spirit of the Fomor."

Then the Dagda, the All-Father, said wearily:

"The powers that you boast of I must lend you all by my good self, for I am a god and equal to all of you!"

"Yes indeed it is you who are the good God," roared Lugh and the whole assembly gave a great shout of laughter for they loved the portly Dagda and his ways.

Then Lugh spoke to the whole army and put strength in them, so that every warrior felt within him the spirit of a king and a hero.

2. THE TRACK OF DAGDA'S CLUB

Now it was the seventh day before Samain of that year and the assembly adjourned as was the custom.

The Dagda had a house in Glenn Etin in the north of the country and he agreed with Lugh that he should spy out the Fomor, who lived there, and report their numbers.

On his way, at the river Uinnus, he saw a woman of great beauty bathing; nine tresses falling across her shoulders. The Dagda stopped, but the woman looked back at him without shame.

DAGDA AND THE
W62MAN OF UINNIUS

DAGDA AGUS BAN NA HABHAINN

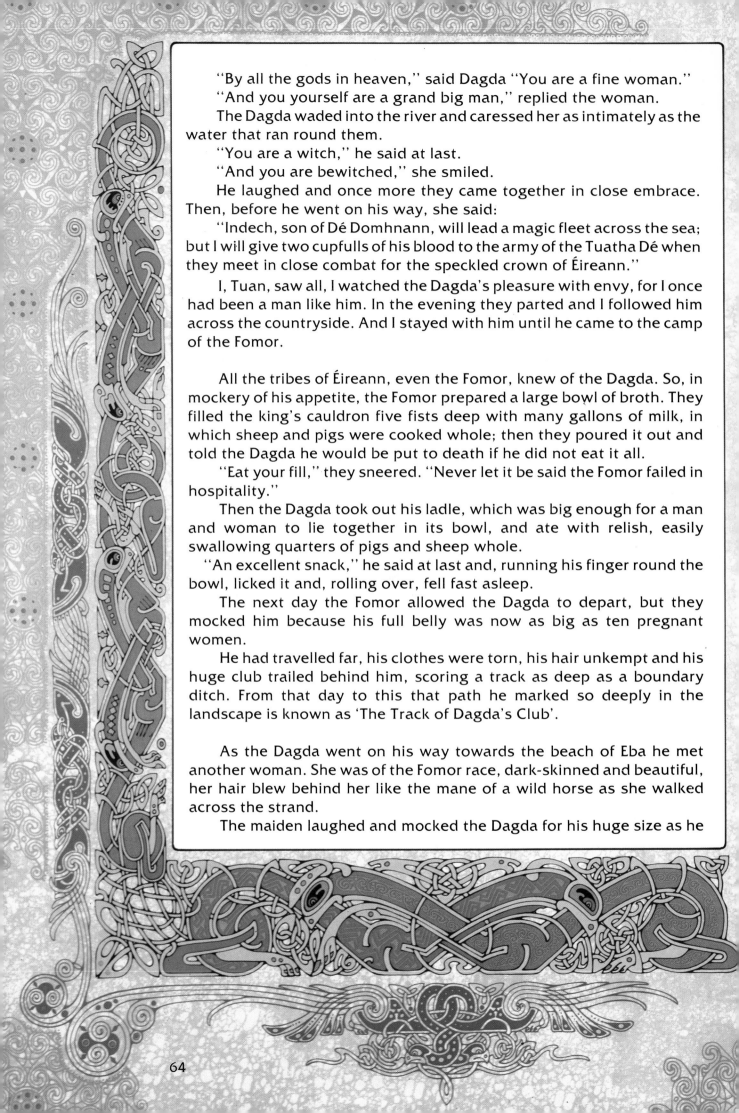

"By all the gods in heaven," said Dagda "You are a fine woman."

"And you yourself are a grand big man," replied the woman.

The Dagda waded into the river and caressed her as intimately as the water that ran round them.

"You are a witch," he said at last.

"And you are bewitched," she smiled.

He laughed and once more they came together in close embrace. Then, before he went on his way, she said:

"Indech, son of Dé Domhnann, will lead a magic fleet across the sea; but I will give two cupfulls of his blood to the army of the Tuatha Dé when they meet in close combat for the speckled crown of Éireann."

I, Tuan, saw all, I watched the Dagda's pleasure with envy, for I once had been a man like him. In the evening they parted and I followed him across the countryside. And I stayed with him until he came to the camp of the Fomor.

All the tribes of Éireann, even the Fomor, knew of the Dagda. So, in mockery of his appetite, the Fomor prepared a large bowl of broth. They filled the king's cauldron five fists deep with many gallons of milk, in which sheep and pigs were cooked whole; then they poured it out and told the Dagda he would be put to death if he did not eat it all.

"Eat your fill," they sneered. "Never let it be said the Fomor failed in hospitality."

Then the Dagda took out his ladle, which was big enough for a man and woman to lie together in its bowl, and ate with relish, easily swallowing quarters of pigs and sheep whole.

"An excellent snack," he said at last and, running his finger round the bowl, licked it and, rolling over, fell fast asleep.

The next day the Fomor allowed the Dagda to depart, but they mocked him because his full belly was now as big as ten pregnant women.

He had travelled far, his clothes were torn, his hair unkempt and his huge club trailed behind him, scoring a track as deep as a boundary ditch. From that day to this that path he marked so deeply in the landscape is known as 'The Track of Dagda's Club'.

As the Dagda went on his way towards the beach of Eba he met another woman. She was of the Fomor race, dark-skinned and beautiful, her hair blew behind her like the mane of a wild horse as she walked across the strand.

The maiden laughed and mocked the Dagda for his huge size as he approached. But the Dagda felt great lust for this woman and blocked her path. She pushed him aside so he rolled back on his bare buttocks and vomited up his Fomor meal. When he tried to get up the woman sat on him, laughing. He said:

"Woman let me get up and go on my way."

"On one condition I will," said the woman. "If you carry me on your back to my father's house."

"Who is your father?"

"My father is Indech, son of Dé Domnann," she answered and pulled him down again so this time he fell on his great belly.

"Will you carry me?" she asked.

"I cannot," said the Dagda, "for it is my taboo never to carry anyone who cannot tell my name."

"What is your name then?"

"Fer Benn, the Man of Horn."

"That is too a great name for you," laughed the woman and mocked him:

"Man of Horn, coarse stomached, pot-bellied,
Bare-arsed, limp-limbed, big-balled;
Who empties his huge stomach on the beach;
Leaves the imprint of his belly on the sand
And the track of his long limb on the land."

"Hold your tongue woman," said the Dagda, "I will do as you ask."

As he laboured under the weight of the maiden, his testicles and enormous penis dragged on the ground. The girl was inflamed by the sight of him and she stepped down, stripped herself and glanced sidelong at him.

And the Dagda took the dark maid in his arms and made love to her with such passion that the hollowed bed of their coming together can be seen to this very day on the strand of Eba; it is known as 'The Bed of the Coupling'.

Then the woman, maid no longer, asked Dagda what his purpose was in the land of the Fomor.

"I have come to learn of the coming of Balor and of the host of Indech your father, for the men of Éireann wish to do battle with them."

"Surely you will not fight in battle," asked the woman, "for you will certainly lose against the powerful Fomor."

"I am a great god among my race," said the Dagda, "and I will bring them good fortune in the war to come."

"You shall not go." replied the woman, "for I will become a stone that will block the entrance to every ford you come to."

DAGDA AND
THE DAUGHTER OF INDECH.

DAƷDA AƷUS INION INDECH.

"I will thrust my way through you," said Dagda.

"I shall become an oaktree and block all your ways."

"I shall break the boughs of the tree, cleave its trunk with my axe," replied Dagda. Then the daughter of Indech, King of the Fomor, said to the Dagda:

"I will tell you what you want to know. The Fomor will come in their black-sailed ships and land at Mag Scéne. At their head will be Indech, the king, and Balor, the Wizard Lord. But it is I who will lead them and, for the sake of you, I will delay them with my magic until the men of Éireann can be gathered in one place, the pillared plain of Moy Tura."

3. THE STORY OF LUGH

At Samain's end Dagda returned to Royal Tara and told all that had befallen him. The news that Balor himself was to accompany the army of Indech filled the warriors with foreboding. Nuada of the Silver Arm was the first to speak:

"This is worse than we expected, for our armies are well matched with the Fomor, but our druids and sorcerers are as helpless as new born babes against Balor of the Evil Eye, the most powerful sorcerer the world has ever known. It was he who caused the drowning of the paradise kingdom of Hy-Brasyl. Our ancestors were persecuted by him and forced to leave the sacred soil of Éireann. Now he comes to destroy us for ever."

Then Lugh, the Shining One, The White Warrior of Legend, rose and spoke to the assembly:

"I am the Il-Dána, Master of All Arts. This is my story:

"Long before I was born, Balor caused his druids to foretell the future and the cause of his death, so that he might avoid it.

"He lived on the Island of The Tower of Glass. All the world paid frightened tribute to him.

"The druids foretold that he would die by the hand of the son of his daughter Ethne, so he imprisoned her in a tower guarded by many women and ordered that no man should come near her.

"Ethne grew up a beautiful maiden. Sometimes, as she stood gazing from her tower, she saw the ships of men pass by, and sometimes she dreamt of a man with shining hair, but her women would give her no answer when she spoke of her dreams.

"Day by day she increased in beauty, but Balor was unafraid, so fast prisoned she was, and he continued in his cruel and greedy domination of the world. He feared only one race, and that was the race of Nemed.

ETHNE, MOTHER OF LUGH.
MEÁN FÓMHAIR · 79

ethne, Máthair Lúgh
JIM FITZPATRICK

69

When they returned to Éireann in their magic flying ships, he resolved to avoid confrontation until they were weakened by wars and fierce taxes.

"But before the First Battle of Moy Tura, Cian of the Tuatha Dé, who had heard of the beautiful maid, sought out the Tower of Glass, after gaining the help of a powerful druidess, Biróg of the Mountain.

"The druidess dressed Cian in princess's clothes and brought him to the Island of the Tower of Glass. Biróg called to the women who waited on the princess and said she had brought a princess shipwrecked on the shore, a noble maid who begged for shelter. The women did not wish to offend a princess of the Tuatha Dé and the powerful druidess, so they admitted them to the tower. Then Biróg caused the women to fall asleep and Cian put aside his women's clothes and went to Ethne and lay with her. Ethne recognised the face of her dreams and returned his love. Then Cian and Biróg left once more on a blast of wind.

"When Balor found his daughter was with child, he was full of rage and fear. But in his cunning he sealed his alliance with the Tuatha Dé by promising his daughter to Cian. However, when the child was born he ordered that it be wrapped in cloth and thrown into the sea. The baby was given to a waiting woman who had lost her own child in still-birth, so she changed the dead child for the living one and threw that into the sea, so that the all-seeing eye of Balor was satisfied and saw the drowning.

"The infant was brought to Cian by Biróg the druidess and Cian gave him to be fostered by Tailltu, daughter of the King of Spain and queen of the Fir Bolg.

"Thus it was that I, Lugh, was born and reared and trained in all the Arts and Sciences. And so it is told that Balor will die by my hand."

The Tuatha Dé Danann took great heart from the words of Lugh, the Il-Dána, and were encouraged by the belief that they had found at last a champion, an equal match for the terrible Balor of the Evil Eye.

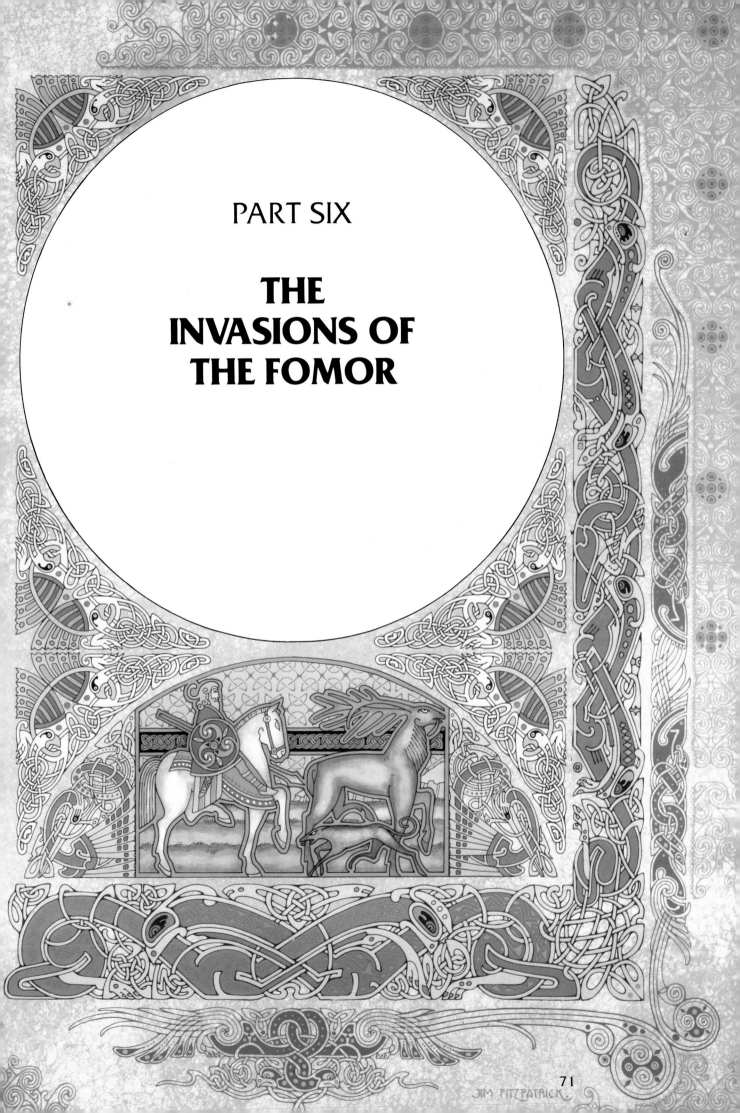

PART SIX

THE INVASIONS OF THE FOMOR

JIM FITZPATRICK

THE INVASIONS OF THE FOMOR

1. BREAS LANDS WITH HIS ARMY OF FOMOR

While the warriors of the Tuatha Dé sat listening to the words of Lugh, messengers came to the fortress of Dagda at Brú na Bóann near Tara with word of the landing of Breas together with the Fomor fleet at Connacht.

The ruler of that part of Éireann was Bove the Red, son of the Dagda, who sent to his father for help against the invading enemy.

Dagda hastened to the assembly and told them of the Fomor invasion under the leadership of Breas, their dishonoured king, and how they were laying waste the territory of his son; torturing and stealing from his people.

"I will meet them as quickly as I can," said Lugh, "but I will need more men so that I can destroy them before the coming of Balor."

"We cannot help you," said Nuada sombrely. "You must fight alone for we need to save every one of our warriors. Our army cannot be divided before the great battle; we can afford no more losses. They come to avenge themselves against you who have slain their kinsmen. I cannot give my kinsmen to settle a quarrel that is not mine."

At Nuada's words Lugh turned angrily away and strode out of the assembly. Then, mounting his magic white horse, he rode from Tara into the dawn.

On his journey westwards Lugh stopped at the fortress of his father, Cian. There he was met by both his father and his brothers Cú and Cethren. Already prepared for battle, they were eager to join Lugh in his plan to destroy the first Fomor invaders.

"We will join with you and each of us will ward off from you a hundred of the savage Fomor warriors," they said.

"Your hearts are brave and generous," answered Lugh, "but the help I need most is this: hasten through the country and call up the riders of the Shí, the Faerie Host, to aid me in my wars."

Whilst Cian, Cú and Cethren set off for the fairy-mounds of Éireann, Lugh rode straight across the country and mountainside until he reached the plain where the Fomor were encamped, heaped around with their plunder and hostages. Lugh paused before the camp. Behind the heavy stockade fluttered silken banners; shields and helmets hanging

LÚGH RIDES TO BATTLE

MARCAÍOCHT LÚGH CHUN CATH

DEIRE FÓMHAIR · 79

JIM FITZPATRICK

before the bright coloured tents caught the rays of the sun.

I, Tuan, sailed high over the Fomor camp among storm clouds that drove across the sun. Sunlight and shadow chequered the plain, and, as I watched, a rainbow formed a great arch round Lugh, the Il-Dána, as he stood on the brow of the hill. Slowly he lifted his shield and sword and, in answer, a beam of light broke through the dark clouds and dressed the hero in all the colours of the world; the boss of his shield and the blade of his sword seemed to burn with fire.

In all the time of my life as man, beast and bird, I had never seen the like of such a hero and I knew that none who came after would equal him.

It was at that same time that Breas the Beautiful rose and looked across the land. He saw the brightness that was Lugh and asked:

"It is strange that the sun should rise in the west today. What omen is this?"

"It is a sign of ill fortune; it is the radiance of a warrior without equal," his druids replied.

Then, in a blinding light, Lugh rode his horse Aonvarr towards the Fomor. As he approached he again raised his sword and shield high in the air and the earth trembled beneath him.

Breas and the Fomor were struck dumb at the sight of the beauty and strength of Lugh, far greater even than Breas at his prime. They wondered too when Lugh saluted them:

"How does it come to pass that one such as you should salute us who are your enemy?"

"I salute you as my kinsmen," replied Lugh, "the blood of both the Dé Danann and the Fomor flows in my veins, for I am the son of Ethne, the daughter of Balor, your overlord. I come in peace to ask you to return to the men of Connacht all the milch cows and the other plunder you have taken from them."

"May ill-luck follow you," said the chieftain of the Fomor, "and may all your cows be dry." And others spoke in like strain.

Then Lugh, angered by their insults, turned from them determined to revenge himself against their discourtesy.

During the night of the next day the Fairie riders of the Shí came to help Lugh, the Il-Dána. With them came the army of Bove the Red, son of the Dagda, numbering twenty-nine hundred Dé Danann men. The time of the Battle of the Il-Dána had come.

2. THE DEFEAT OF BREAS THE BEAUTIFUL

At dawn of the next day, Lugh's army crashed down on Breas's camp like a tidal wave.

Lugh's men raised their spears high above their helmets and made closed shield-walls against their enemies. The Fomor hurled their spears at random, and Lugh's side easily deflected them with their long shields. When the Fomor warriors were in total disarray and confusion, many weaponless, the Il-Dána's army seemed to retreat, still facing their enemy shoulder to shoulder.

The Fomor reassembled themselves and made a fierce charge at the centre of their enemy's rank. Instead of standing firm, the middle of Lugh's army moved deliberately backwards, luring the Fomor warriors after them. The left and right flank advanced and closed behind the enemy, cutting off their retreat and preventing reinforcements from arriving.

Then, with a wild war-cry, the invincible hero, Lugh, plunged through the centre of the trapped Fomor host. Behind him followed the Shí, the Faerie Host, riding in terrible silence on their winged steeds. From the silver feet of their horses there rose a mist that dimmed the dark Fomor eyes, so that they did not know whether they struck down friend or foe. Rank after rank of the Fomor fell before the onslaught of Lugh and his magical companions.

But the Fomor druids countered Lugh's magical mists with icy winds and blinding hail showers, which broke up the Dé Danann battle formations and drowned the shouted instructions of their commanders.

Regaining their courage, the scattered Fomor reassembled at the western end of the plain. Breas had noted the strategy of the Dé Danann commanders and he instructed his troops to keep well together and to fight in pairs, one soldier defending his partner while he delivered death blows to the Dé Danann warriors. Breas further ordered that the Fomor cavalry should divide into two formations and wait until the Dé Danann army was split by the onslaught of the foot soldiers, then advance quickly and attack the Dé Danann hosts on both flanks.

The Fomor soldiers were heartened by Breas's words and, keeping well together, made a savage charge against the enemy. Bove the Red, son of Dagda, and his men were the first to meet and fall beneath their bloody onslaught. The Fomor left Bove for dead, but the faithful bodyguard of Dagda's noble son dragged him out of the battlefield and tended his near fatal wounds.

Then Lugh withdrew to the top of the hill, taking his magical riders with him. He called to the Dé Danann army to gather round him. By magic the Dé Dananns alone heard his rallying cry and, as they ran to rejoin their leader, the Fomor's soldiers thought they had won the field and that the Dé Dananns were retreating. Thus they fell easy prey to Lugh's attack. He and his Faerie riders plunged first among the Fomor ranks and made way for the advance of the Dé Dananns who had formed a solid phalanx, bristling with spears and covered with a shell of shields. Terrible slaughter followed; the screams of the dying mixed with war-cries. Those warriors who remained alive, fought, not on earth, but on a field of bodies of both foe and kinsmen slippery with blood.

Lugh had other business. Hacking his way through the Fomor ranks he sought out Breas, their leader. The Il-Dána easily recognised Breas by his golden hair and his beauty, but, as he lifted his blood-stained sword to attack him, Breas spoke:

"We share the same blood equally, the blood of the Tuatha Dé and the Fomor, so let there be peace between us, for no man born of woman can resist your magical powers. In return for my life I give you my word that I will not fight against you in the coming battle that Balor is sure to mount to avenge this defeat."

"Balor and Indech are already nearing these shores with their dark fleet," answered Lugh.

"Then you and the race of Nemed are surely lost," said Breas.

"That the Fates will decide," said Lugh, "I am their instrument. The order of events is pre-ordained. I will spare your life, but do not face me in battle again!"

When the Fomor saw their leader, Breas, captured and disarmed by

Lugh, they too asked for peace.

"I have no wish to kill any of you," said the Il-Dána, "for you are of my father's blood. Return the spoils of your conquests to the people of the Tuatha Dé and leave this land in peace."

So it was that Breas and his army were defeated.

I, Tuan the eagle, rejoiced in the victory of my race; but my heart went out also to Breas the Beautiful, once a hero of the First Battle of Moy Tura, now a king dishonoured, sad and desperate. I knew that history reveals the true difference between fools and heroes; and I wept for the fate of Breas the Beautiful, once so full of promise, but betrayed by an uncertain heart and a grudging spirit.

3. THE ARMIES MARCH TO MOY TURA

For nine days before the coming of the Fomor fleet the gods sent showers of stars blazing across the night-sky and strange lights leapt in the north.

I, Tuan, was filled with foreboding, for I felt certain that these omens presaged more death and destruction for the men of Éireann. As I drifted high over the headlands of Scéne I saw Balor's fleet of black and green sailed ships crowd the ocean beneath me.

When he heard the news of the arrival of Balor's fleet, Nuada sent for his advisers, for something else hung heavily on his mind:

"We must keep Lugh, the Il-Dána, from the battle till the last, for his death would be a grievous blow to us." So it was decided to leave the Il-Dána at Tara until his skills were most needed. The nine sons of Manannan Mac Lir were left to guard him.

The Dé Danann army marched across the country for four days, until they reached the eastern side of Loch Arrow, where they set up camp and began to prepare for battle against the Fomor.

"Here we will make our stand," said Nuada, "on the battlefield of Moy Tura, where so many of our heroes fell in our greatest victory. Let these lichen-covered pillars serve as our battle props and remind us of the bravery of our dead champions. May the Second Battle of Moy Tura, the Plain of Pillars, go as well for us as the first."

Then Mórfhis, the druid, rolled the twelve mountains of Éireann across the plain. The cup-bearers dried up the great lakes and rivers. Figol put a hold on their enemy's urine and caused rains of fire to fall on them as they advanced. The Badb haunted their nights, and by day caused the trees, stones and earth to rise up against them.

But for every two tricks of the Dé Danann, Balor had three, and so the Fomor army soon reached the plain of Moy Tura.

4. THE VISION REVEALED

The night before the day of battle, Nuada prayed to his gods on the high mountain overlooking the preparations on the plain of Moy Tura.

Nuada felt fate heavy upon him as he looked down on the two great hosts and their fires as bright and numerous, it seemed, as the stars above.

At last the rising sun broke through the darkness and fringed the mountains with gold. Colour returned to the world and the morning was filled with bird-song. It seemed to Nuada that he gazed on homeland and paradise for the last time. Then the king remembered the dream of his delirium. He recognised now the meaning and truth of his vision.

The dream had told him that he would regain kingship of Éireann. It had given him an arm of silver. He remembered the two hosts of silent stones and the two armies; one set of stones was ranged in perfect formation like the Dé Danann force, the other set was as confused and uneven as the slow-assembling armies of the Fomor.

Nuada knew now his past, his present and his future; he saw the gates of the great palace of the Otherworld open to receive him. He raised his shield to the sun and lifted his Sword of Light so that all the brightness of the morning ran along its blade:

"Lámh Láidir Abú," he cried, "Lámh Láidir Abú

I am Nuada son of the sun

I am the Silver-Arm."

Then Nuada lowered his sword and, resting against a stone that stood high over the plain, whistled for his horse, and pulling down his pack put on his armour. The Second Battle of Moy Tura was about to begin.

5. THE FIRST DAY OF BATTLE

The Tuatha Dé marched in perfect battle order. As they approached the Fomor camp they beat their shields with their swords and shouted out their war-cries, while their druids, standing on stones overlooking the plain, made their war-horns and boar-headed trumpets wail and roar with supernatural sound. Their wizards lit bonfires and chanted their

THE EVE OF BATTLE.

NUADA ROIMH AN CATH

81

JIM FITZPATRICK

war-spells. The Badb, in their guise of black witches, ran towards the Fomor brandishing their smoking torches and screaming imprecations. So terrible was the sound of the Dé Danann army, that the Fomor, fierce fighters though they were, felt their skins crawl with fear.

I, Tuan, watched the advance of the Tuatha Dé Danann across the plain of Moy Tura, with awe and anguish. I remembered the terrible bloodshed of the First Battle, which had seen the eclipse of the Fir Bolg power and the dawning of the glory of the Tuatha Dé Danann. I knew that the second battle would be equally decisive and out of death and humiliation there would emerge new heroes, new history.

When the Tuatha Dé were more than three quarters of the way towards the Fomor camp, a wild war-cry echoed across the field. Indech, son of Dé Domhnann, and his horse-warriors, came from the camp and as they charged the Dé Danann flanks, a crowd of fierce young Fomor warriors attacked the Dé Danann centre with raised swords and short spears.

With a great clash the shields of the two armies met and the hills echoed with cries of frenzy and anguish as the Dé Danann centre caved in before such a terrible onslaught. But although the Fomor had cut a bloody gap in their centre, the Dé Danann line absorbed the initial shock and stood firm again while, from behind the front lines, spearmen sent showers of javelins into the Fomor army. The warriors in the Fomor centre and rear could do nothing but endure the hail of poisoned shafts, while they pressed forward to take their place in the broken front rank.

Slowly the front shield-wall of the Dé Danann retreated, luring the Fomor warriors into a battle trap. But the Dé Danann flanks, upon which the success of the strategy depended, were under such fierce attack from the Fomor cavalry, that they could do nothing to help the front line and so, for a time, the battle raged like a tumultuous sea as warrior engaged with warrior in fights to the death.

So great was the ferocity and press of the battle, that the bodies of men who were mortally wounded, or even dead, remained upright with no room to fall, so that many a warrior, blinded with blood, engaged in a futile duel with a lifeless body.

6. THE VICTORY OF OCTRIALLACH AND THE DEATH OF RUADAN

It was then, at the height of the battle-chaos, that Octriallach, son of Indech, King of the Fomor, made his powerful onset on the line of the Tuatha Dé. In dazzling battle array he made for their right flank where Cassmael, a prince of the Tuatha Dé, led the line.

The two heroes singled each other out for combat, Cassmael first striking Octriallach with his short thrusting spear. The son of Indech parried the blow and his opponent's weapon snapped against his shield. Then Cassmael drew his silver-studded sword and, with a great war-cry, charged Octriallach.

The encounter of the two men was so fierce that both of the exhausted armies paused to watch.

Octriallach chose to fight with his powerful battle-axe and as Cassmael brought his sword down on his shield, the young Fomor brought his axe down with so strong a blow that both Cassmael's shield and breastplate were shattered. The Dé Danann hero fell to his knees with a groan and as the son of Indech split his helmet open with a second stroke of his axe, Cassmael fell to the earth, and in his death agony clutched at the grass which his own young blood had stained.

As the young Dé Danann yielded up his life, so the battle resumed in all its earnestness and previous confusion and it was not until sunset that the two armies pulled apart.

For two whole days the armies of the Fomor and the Tuatha Dé Danann fought without any decisive result. But one thing puzzled the Fomor and that was that, although their own weapons were blunted and broken, the Tuatha Dé seemed to have their spears and swords magically renewed. This was because Goibhnu, the smith, Lúchta the carpenter and Créidne the brazier, true to the promise they had made earlier to their king, Nuada, joined their skills in repairing their army's weapons as soon as they were broken.

The other thing that worried the Fomor was that, while their own wounded either died or lay grievously sick, the Dé Danann casualties seemed to recover from their wounds overnight. This was because of the promise Dian-cécht, the healer, had made earlier and that was that he would take the wounded men and bathe them in the Well of Healing at Slaine, west of Moy Tura and then, with the power of his spells and incantations and the healing balms he made with his secret knowledge of herbs, make the heroes whole again.

Then the Fomor sent Ruadan, son of Breas, to the camp of the Tuatha Dé to seek out Goibhnu the smith and kill him, so that his army would be without weapons. Ruadan went to Goibhnu's forge and, being of Dé Danann blood, had no difficulty in entering. He asked Créidne and Lúchta to put a spear together for him. Then he turned and threw the spear at Goibhnu, wounding him. But Goibhnu pulled the spear from his side and hurled it against Ruadan who died in the arms of his Dé Danann mother, Brigit, wife of Breas.

All this took place while Lugh paced the Hall of Royal Tara waiting for his time to come. When he heard of the death of the young prince Cassmael, he resolved to join the fight the next day, for he knew the third day would be the decisive one. On that day Balor and Nuada would meet fact to face as was the custom and no one but he, the Il-Dána, could outmatch the wizard-lord of the Fomor.

So it was that Lugh cast a sleeping spell over his foster brothers who guarded him, and set out alone for Moy Tura to aid his people in their fight for justice and peace.

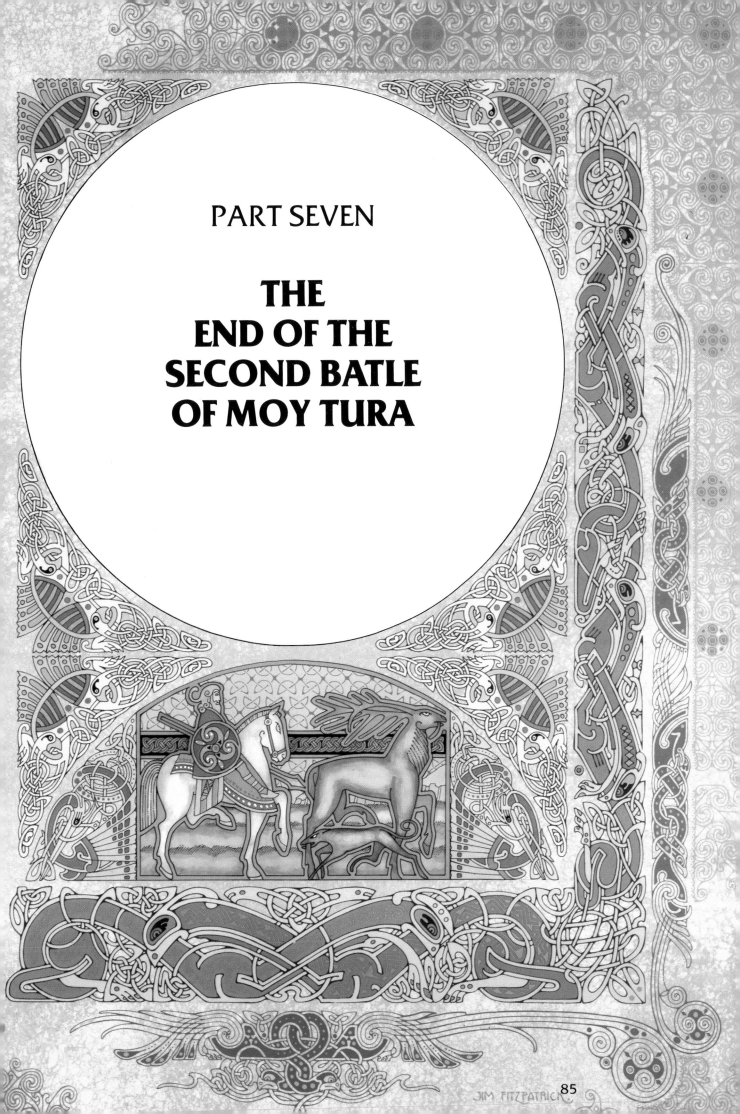

PART SEVEN

THE
END OF THE
SECOND BATLE
OF MOY TURA

THE END OF THE SECOND BATTLE OF MOY TURA

1. THE ARMIES ASSEMBLE ON THE THIRD DAY

The third day saw the alignment of the sun upon the solar wheel atop the Bricklieve Mountains. It shone on the greatest gathering of heroes and warriors in the history of Éireann.

The armies of the Tuatha Dé made the first move that morning. In dazzling battalions they moved across the white dew; their silk-embroidered pennants fluttered above their bronze armour and shining helmets. As they neared the centre of the plain the lines split up into separate war groups arranged as a huge open backed square; each side composed of three separate smaller squares, for three times three made up their sacred number; nine.

The leaders of the three front groups were in the centre; Nuada of the Silver Arm and his sons, and around him his Scythian bodyguard, clad in black armour and horse-hair plumed helmets; then to the right of the king stood Dagda and his sons Aengus, Mac Og and Bove the Red; to the left stood Ogma, brother of Dagda and master tactician of the armies of the Tuatha Dé. To Ogma the battle was a game of chess, he had meticulously planned the opening strategies to counter the wild ferocity of the Fomor with cold cunning.

Behind the battle-lines the sorcerers of the Tuatha Dé, led by the wizard, Mórfhís, watched for the appointed signals and kindled their fires on the hills. The Badb waited with them: Macha, Mórrigan and Nemain.

The fateful confrontation with Balor was at hand.

The Fomor had gathered in a long deep line at the northern end of Loch Arrow in front of their camp. Every one of them was heavily armed and cunning, menacing and pitiless as the marauding beasts of mountain and forest.

NUADA AIRZEDLÁMH

NUADA OF THE SILVER ARM.

MÁRTA 80

JIM FITZPATRICK

THE TUATHA DÉ ASSEMBLE FOR BATTLE.

CRUINNIN NA TUATHA DÉ CHUN CATH
JIM FITZPATRIC

The Fomor army was led first by Balor of the Evil Eye, reputed immortal leader of their tribes. The next in command were:

Indech; King and Battle Commander,

Elathan the Immortal; sea lord and father of Breas,

Octriallach; Champion of his race, son of Indech.

Breas the Beautiful, once King of the Tuatha Dé Danann, had sworn to take no part in the battle, for he did not wish to break the promise he had made to Lugh.

The Fomor army looked dark and sinister opposite the bright and glittering ranks of the Tuatha Dé Danann. At a signal from Indech, the Fomor army moved forward from their earthworks in a powerfully packed line flanked by horse-warriors. From behind the Fomor army rose the flames of Balor's sacrificial fires, which he fed with flesh hacked from Dé Danann warriors during the previous day's slaughter. Then, with a great shout, the Fomor charged in a wild, disorganised mass.

Dagda gave the signal with his leather-tongued horn and the Tuatha Dé army stopped dead, and suddenly raised a wall of shields and bristling spears before their enemies.

The impetus of the Fomor charge impaled their vanguard on the Dé Danann weapons, so that the rearguard slipped and fell over their bloody corpses, unable even to wield their swords in the fearful crush.

The phalanx of the Tuatha Dé was well able to contain them, but the sheer weight of bodies caused the shield wall to buckle, while the flanks commanded by Dagda and Ogma had to bear the brunt of the cavalry led by Indech.

Now, at another signal from Dagda's war-horn, the front line of each square lowered their shields and knelt behind them, embedding their spears in the earth at an angle aimed at the enemy. Thus the Dé Dananns held the Fomor at bay while the second line of warriors hacked with swords and axes at any of the dark enemy who cut their way through the first line.

The slaughter was terrible; men and horses screamed as they twisted, impaled upon spears. But as the will of the Fomor wavered, the Dé Danann phalanx drove forward, carving out a path before it. In a desperate attempt to save his men, Indech, King of the Fomor, called on his gods; and his deep throated cry urged the cavalry straight towards the centre of the Dé Danann warriors, breaking the wall of shields. It was to Indech's sword that Ogma, brother of Dagda, fell that day, and his loss was to be lamented long after by his kinsmen.

2. THE DEATH OF INDECH, KING OF THE FOMOR

With wild cries, the Fomor hurled themselves on the disordered Dé Danann centre. There was chaos as men from both sides were trampled underfoot by the terrified horses.

In the centre square Nuada's bodyguard fought fiercely. On either side the Dé Danann formations held their own and slowly closed up to Nuada's shattered centre, while the other middle squares closed with them. Nuada regrouped his warriors around a great standing-stone raised to the memory of a fallen hero in the First Battle of Moy Tura and his swarthy Scythian bodyguard formed a battle pen around him.

Still Indech fought on, forcing the Dé Dananns into a hard packed mass, while Octriallach, his son, launched a fresh attack on Dagda's men, pushing them back again into the battle mêlée. Although Indech had little sense of strategy and relied on the brute force and battle frenzy of his men, his forces wreaked terrible havoc on the Dé Danann lines.

At last Nuada raised his Sword of Light to catch the life energy from his father, the Sun God, and cried:

"Help me put an end to this slaughter of our youth."

With these words he charged his golden steed past his dark skinned Scythian guards and stood face to face with Indech, the Fomor King. With one accord the two armies moved apart so that their two kings should have space for the final combat.

As Indech wheeled on his great black mare, Nuada plunged his sword into the creature's underbelly and, with a twist of the wrist, disembowelled it. Before Indech could struggle from beneath his

stricken mount, Nuada was standing over him, sword point at his throat:

"End this battle in our favour or this breath shall be your last."

"Never," replied Indech. "There is too much bitterness between our races to be settled by the life or death of one man."

"So be it," said Nuada and with one stroke severed Indech's head from his shoulders.

The Fomor king's black hair fell over his olive skinned face and he gave a long sigh as his life left him in a crimson river. Dark clouds hid the sun and rain fell like tears.

I, Tuan the eagle, had to bear the pain of all men in my heart and I felt the anguish and shame of Octriallach, son of Indech, as he watched Nuada strip his father's body of its ceremonial battle armour. I, too, felt the grief and bitterness of the Fomor people at the death of their king. I knew that their wizard overlord, Balor, would wreak terrible revenge for the loss of his battle-commander.

3. NUADA'S BATTLE WITH THE DEMON

The sacrificial fires kindled by Balor of the Evil Eye were now fed by the bodies of the Fomor dead, while the heads of the slain Dé Dananns were piled around the altar of Crom-Crúach, the Worm God.

Long wax tapers were set around the pyramid of severed heads and runes and symbols chalked in a circle. Red flames and smoke, smelling of death, rolled across the plain towards the Dé Danann army.

Balor stood, black cloaked, his hands raised towards the heavens and behind him towered the shadow of Crom-Crúach, the Worm God.

In the centre of the plain, Nuada rested on his chequered red cloak, within the battle pen his Scythian bodyguards had made with their stakes and spears. Some of his army still fought on to settle old scores or to avenge lost kinsmen. The rest, exhausted, made a camp where they awaited another Fomor attack. But their fears were groundless; the Fomor, grieved and demoralised by the death of Indech, had no stomach for fighting.

As Nuada slept, the darkness of Balor's evil hung in the air; all creatures hid from it, every man's heart grew cold, Dé Danann and Fomor alike.

Once again, as at the first Battle of Moy Tura, the standing stones began to shriek. Nuada was woken by the terrible wailing. All knew that battle-prowess was in vain now that Balor had entered the fray.

Nuada called for his faithful horse and to his son Lughai he said: "This is the testing time. Ride and fetch the Il-Dána."

Then, with a great cry, he drew his Sword of Light and pressed it to the red jewel set in his helmet; a quivering fire ran down the rune-engraven blade so the silver turned to crimson.

As his sword came alive, a huge shadow passed overhead and the King of the Tuatha Dé realised this was the day for which all his life had been the preparation: the time when he must pit his strength and magic against the arcane powers of the reputedly immortal Balor. Fear chilled him. The ultimate price he might have to pay would be his soul itself, which would be fed to the demon god, Crom-Crúach.

He swung his magical sword and cut a swathe through the dark mists. The path of hope gave comfort to his men. Again and again Nuada scythed away the darkness, so that in the end he had cleared Balor's mists and the centre of the plain was as bright as day, though terrible storms raged round it.

But soon Nuada felt the chill of fear again. Once more the shadow of the Worm God towered over him, eager for his spirit.

Nuada called on the Badb to help him ward off that monstrous star-born creature. The three war witches drove their fiery war chariot into the core of the demon, blinding its eye with their torches.

The Worm God roared in anger and clawed aside the chariot of the Badb, tearing the head from the child-witch, Macha, and impaling the beautiful Nemain. Mórrigan, seeing the dreadful deaths of her sisters, changed herself into a raven and hid in the hazel groves beyond Moy Tura.

I, Tuan, lamented the loss of Macha and Nemain, for the breaking of their sisterhood was a cruel blow to the children of Nemed. The Badb, the triple war-goddesses, no longer existed but had passed from life into legend; now only the words of the story teller could conjure up their beauty in the hearts of his listeners.

As I watched I saw the terrible shadow crouch closer over Nuada. Out of the darkness of his terror the king raised his Sword of Light and again held it against his bull-horned helmet. This time the crimson light infused his silver arm and gave him a magical strength of limb.

Then a great battle frenzy seized Nuada, king of the Tuatha Dé Danann, and he rose in all the splendour of his father, the Sun God, up into the sky where Balor's demon god awaited him. With his Sword of Light Nuada severed the tentacles of darkness; whirling his weapon in fiery crescents he lopped off claws and limbs from the huge and terrible creature which filled the heavens with its swirling knotted coils.

But, even as he seemed to destroy the monster, it changed in shape and substance, dissolving into some foul broth which boiled and clotted into myriad forms which writhed and knotted together in dripping slime. Even the Sword of Light was powerless against the bubbling source of evil which would never be quenched until the end of the world.

Nuada felt cold grip his heart and in his mind nightmare visions of unnamable demons and forbidden gods became obscene reality. At last he knew there was no hope of victory; all that was left to him was to bear witness to the life and truth that he had managed to forge during his brief time on Earth. And so, as the demon slowly engulfed him, he cried again and again to his God the Sun to give light and warmth to his people, the Tuatha Dé Danann, the children of Nemed, so that their hearts would be brave, their spirits leap high, and their children's children run free in the green homeland, their own country of Éireann.

4. THE DEATH OF NUADA OF THE SILVER ARM

High above the plain of Moy Tura, Lugh the Il-Dána, paused with his faerie host, the Riders of the Shí.

"It was well that we left when we did," he said to Lughai, son of Nuada, "If I had waited for the summons, I would have come too late. We have arrived in time to save our side though we must pay a high price for this delay. Had I been the head of the army on the first day, we might have settled this affair without such terrible slaughter."

Then with a great battle-cry, the Il-Dána drew power from the sun and scattered the storm-clouds with a sweep of his sword-arm. A single star shone in the clear sky above him, while the sun sank behind the Bricklieve Mountains and purple shadow clothed the earth.

The fading gold of evening bathed the hero's armour, so that for a moment he shone like a god in the gathering shadows. Then he charged down on to the plain and plunged into the spiralling Fomor mists, driving them back into the hearts of the terrible fires fed on human flesh.

But indeed the Il-Dána was too late to save his king. Above him, drifting silently in the darkening sky, Lugh saw Nuada, a lifeless broken shadow, suspended in the coils of the demon god, Crom Crúach.

Lugh, the Il-Dána, wept at the death of the hero king. But then his cry of grief turned to terrible anger. Balor recognised that the time of his fate was upon him and his black blood ran cold. For the first time he knew mortal fear. He had met his equal.

I, Tuan, also mourned the passing of Nuada of the Silver Arm, greatest king of the Tuatha Dé Danann and I rejoiced that Lugh, the Il-Dána, had come to avenge him. This spirit now hung between heaven and earth, awaiting damnation from Balor or salvation from Lugh.

As I circled the precious shadow of my beloved king, I saw far below me the last great gathering of the Tuatha Dé Danann on the plain of Moy Tura and my spirit rang loud in my heart:

O may yours be the power
The power of the darkness

NUADA AND
THE DEMON OF DEATH.

NUADA AGUS DAEMHAN NA MARBH.

The power of the sun
Hands to deal death
And hands to create.

Make your land leap green
Free from stranger
Be free from foe
Dark dust blown in your wind.

Glory to you Il-Dána
Hero bring pride to our land
So we children of Nemed
May forever run free.

5. THE IL-DÁNA LEADS THE TUATHA DÉ

And so the Tuatha Dé passed across the plain of Moy Tura in one last great battle array.

At the head of the silent army was Lugh, the Il-Dána, Master of All Arts. Behind him was his bodyguard, the sons of Manannan Mac Lir, the Sea God and the Riders of the Shí. To his right strode Dagda and to his left Bove the Red, son of Dagda. They had united to avenge their king and save his soul from the powers of evil.

Facing them, backs to the sun, were the Fomor army, led by Octriallach, son of Indech. On the hill above crouched Balor in his circle of magic and death. Through his magic power the Demon Lord had fought and won victory against his ancient enemy, Nuada. But now the wizard lay exhausted.

All power spent, Balor surrendered himself to the care of his wife Caithleann, and his twelve druids and his sons stood between him and the approaching Dé Danann army.

Looking across the plain he turned and asked:

"What star is that that waits not for the darkness of night?"

"No star," said Caithleann, "but the brightness of the son of your daughter Eithne. Where you are in the darkness of night, he is in the brightness of day."

"Then the light of the day must yield to the coming darkness of night," said Balor.

On the plain below, Lugh rose in his saddle and swung his sword

round so that he seemed to move within a cage of gold. Thus the legendary Il-Dána blazed a way through the darkness of the Fomor.

Then, spurring his horse, Lugh scythed a path through the dark heart of the enemy; heads, limbs and split shields fell around him. The Il-Dána left a river of blood behind him.

The horn of the Dagda once more sounded the attack and with a great roar the two armies met. This time there was no battle strategy. Each of the Dé Danann warriors sought out a Fomor enemy and engaged in single combat so they might personally avenge the death of their king. Many men on both sides lost their lives that day and once more the plain of Moy Tura ran red with warm blood. This was the most terrible day of the battle, for it seemed as if the very forces of good and evil were in conflict, and men's bodies were being lifted and broken by invisible hands.

6. THE LIGHTNING WEAPON OF LUGH

As his armies engaged behind him, the Il-Dána raced on, the golden hooves of his horse treading the darkness to shreds. All fled from his path, wailing with terror.

Past the camp he rode straight up to the sacrificial fires of Balor. As he approached the wizard's bodyguard he reined Aonvarr to a halt. He gazed in wonder at a strange machine towering behind them; a structure of pulleys, derricks, wheels within wheels, and in the centre a single gigantic wheel of purple metal. Within this circle was throned Balor, his evil eye a silver disc in his forehead.

"Balor," cried the Il-Dána, "I have come to take your life."

"Who is this babbling youth?" said Balor to Caithleann his wife.

"He is the Il-Dána," she replied, "the son of your daughter and he has sworn to destroy you."

Then Balor signalled to his druids and said:

"Raise my eyelid that I may see this audacious boy, who is of my own flesh and blood."

No man save Balor alone had ever been able before to raise the lid of the disc of the Evil Eye. But now Balor was so spent and exhausted that he was completely helpless. Because of this, he had commanded his sorcerers to build the huge wooden tower, so that he might still be able to destroy the Il-Dána and the Tuatha Dé with him.

At Balor's word, the great wheels and pulleys began to turn and set the machine in motion, until at last the polished handle slowly raised the engraven lid of the silver eye set deep in Balor's forehead.

Lugh, the Il-Dána, watched with wonder as the Evil Eye of myth and legend was prised open by the labour of the Fomor druids.

Suddenly the eye stared wide and, from deep within it, blazed a flare of white light that pierced the shadows of evening and swept from side to side across the battle-field, destroying everything within its gaze. A thousand warriors fell in that instant, flesh and bone turned to ashes beneath melted armour. Fomor and Dé Danann alike fell before the deadly beam and the very rocks were branded with the shadows of what had once been men.

As the druids wheeled and turned Balor and his Evil Eye in the direction of the Il-Dána, Lugh drew the most powerful of all his weapons from under its cover of waxed ox-hide. This was the Spear of Lightning, which had belonged to Pisear, King of the Persians; a weapon unequalled in the world, a fireball of untold energy, brought to Lugh by the sons of Tuireann to protect him from the Evil Eye. It had been kept under its ox-hide wrappings, soaked wet, because its power was so great that it might destroy even its owner. But now was the time to use it. The Il-Dána drew it and raised it in a long sling above his twin-horned helmet as the scorching beam of the Evil Eye swept round to him. Once more the Il-Dána uttered his great war-cry and, leaping up onto the back of Aonvarr of the Flowing Mane, he balanced there, poised, aiming the fiery Spear of Lightning. The weapon crackled with power and the air was full of thunder as its magic became fully alive. Straight as an arrow it flew, with a flash of white brilliance, which marked its track from Lugh's hand to its target.

It flew straight into the Eye of Balor with an earth-shaking blast. The air was filled with terrible noises; wails, shrieks and the crying of women and

AN DROCHSHÚIL
MARCA·82

THE EVIL EYE

JIM FITZPATRICK

103

children. Great ghostly figures stalked across the mountains, and the sky was full of blazing comets, while a mist of blood crept across the plain.

Thus it was that Balor of the Evil Eye was destroyed by his own grandson, Lugh, the Il-Dána, as had been foretold by his own druids and seers. And so ended the Second Battle of Moy Tura.

Faster than the wind the Il-Dána rode his white horse away from the Evil Eye. The dark robed body of Balor lay face down amidst the wreckage of his tower. Before the light went out of it for ever, his Evil Eye had burned a hole in the earth as deep and wide as the camp of the Fomor, and gradually it filled with icy water from subterranean streams.

The place where Balor, wizard Lord of the Fomor, fell before the Lightning Weapon of Lugh, the Il-Dána, is known as Loch na Súil, the Lake of the Eye and can be found today in the hills to the north of Moy Tura.

I, Tuan, watched with awe as the magnificent Il-Dána rode once more back across that scorched plain. With one stroke of his sword he severed the head of Balor and, holding it high before him, he displayed it to the remnants of the Fomor and the victorious army of the Tuatha Dé.

Then Mórrigan, the last of the war witches, once mistress of Nuada, called to the lost spirit of the king, now free of the power of Balor, and sent it on its way to beyond the stars. An escort of Riders of the Shí accompanied it on its last journey towards the setting sun and, as the warriors of the Tuatha Dé burned the empty bodies of Nuada of the Silver Arm, Ogma, brother of Dagda, Macha and Nemain of the Badb, and all their slain on a great funeral pyre, Mórrigan sang her lament for them all:

> "Be cradled in starlight
> O Dé Danann heroes
> Never again
> Will the world see your like.
>
> Gaze down on Éireann
> The green land you bought
> With your blood and your boldness
> Now glory of myth.
>
> Peace be in your heaven
> And peace on our earth."

7. EPILOGUE

After the Second Battle of Moy Tura, the Tuatha Dé Danann gave the kingship of Éireann to Lugh, the mystical Il-Dána. He was the greatest hero of that illustrious race and is remembered in the legends of his people until this very day. Lughnasa, which means the month of August in the language of his people, commemorates his feats.

Lugh reigned for forty years and he held his court at Naas. When Tailltu, his beloved foster mother, died he built the massive Fort of the Hostages at Royal Tara to her memory, raised a great mound for her, and instituted the Tailltean Games to be held every summer in honour of her. He gave his natural mother Ethne in marriage to Tadg, son of Nuada, and from that royal line came Bran of the Voyages and the hero Finn, leader of the Fianna Éireann.

As for Breas the Beautiful, he gave to the men of Éireann in return for his life, the secrets of the earth he had learned from the Fomor: ploughing, sowing and reaping. The defeated Fomor never dared again to demand tribute from the Tuatha Dé, and their power in this green island was lost forever with the death of Balor of the Evil Eye.

Although he had lost his life in the Second Battle of Moy Tura, Nuada of the Silver Arm was deified by his people and honoured among their Gods. In death he took his rightful place among the heroes of the Otherworld and his name is remembered to this day.

For many years after that great battle, the Tuatha Dé Danann ruled Éireann in peace and prosperity and it was not until the coming of the

Gael that they yielded the sovereignty of this sacred isle.

I, Tuan, sea-eagle, witnessed all these great events through my many lives and remembered them through the many centuries until I was made man again and born as Tuan, son of Carill, King of Ireland.

But although I recovered my human form, I was removed for ever from the careless joys of boyhood and the passions of manhood. My heart was heavy with the burden of history and myth locked within it. My knowledge set me apart from both men and women; and all my life I spent searching for another who might receive my secret treasure and, holding it safe, pass it on to the children of Éireann's future.

In my old age I told my story to the good priest Finnian of the Church of the Bells. It is he and his scribes who preserve it for eternity.

"Tell me Tuan," said Finnian to me on a bright summer's morning "the number of the slain at that great battle?"

"As to the number of slain at the Second Battle of Moy Tura," I said, "it will never be known until we can number the stars in the sky above, or the flakes of snow in winter, or the blades of grass beneath our feet or the horses of Manannan in a stormy sea."

This is their story and mine.

I am Tuan
I am Legend
I am memory turned myth.